MICHAEL BOND was born in Newbury, Berkshire in 1926 and started writing whilst serving in the army during the Second World War. In 1958 the first book featuring his most famous creation, Paddington Bear, was published and many stories of his adventures followed. In 1983 he turned his hand to adult fiction and the detective cum gastronome par excellence Monsieur Pamplemousse was born.

Michael Bond was awarded the OBE in 1997 and in 2007 was made an Honorary Doctor of Letters by Reading University. He is married, with two grown-up children, and lives in London.

By Michael Bond

Monsieur Pamplemousse Afloat

Michael Bond

Allison & Busby Limited
13 Charlotte Mews
London W1T 4EJ
www.allisonandbusby.com

First published in Great Britain by Allison & Busby in 1998.
This paperback edition published by Allison & Busby in 2012.

A CIP catalogue record for this book is available from
the British Library.

10 9 8 7 6 5 4 3 2 1

ISBN 978-0-7490-1134-5

Typeset in 10.8/15.7 pt Century Schoolbook
by Allison & Busby Ltd.

The paper used for this Allison & Busby publication
has been produced from trees that have been legally sourced
from well-managed and credibly certified forests.

Printed and bound by
CPI Group (UK) Ltd, Croydon, CR0 4YY

Monsieur Pamplemousse
Afloat

CHAPTER ONE

It all began early one summer morning when Monsieur Pamplemousse saw a one-legged *Papa Noël* hopping at speed along the Boulevard Haussman as though he had a train to catch – or a sleigh.

In five months time the pavements outside the large department stores further along the *boulevard* would be awash with men in red robes and crepe beards, but in early July . . .

It was such an unusual sight his attention was momentarily diverted from the road ahead.

The man clearly believed in keeping his hand in, for despite the fact that he was in a hurry he couldn't resist stopping to put his arms round a small child, whilst passing the time of day with its mother. (According to Doucette, during Christmas week the priorities were often reversed – especially after a good lunch!)

When Monsieur Pamplemousse concentrated once again on his driving, he realised to his horror that the traffic lights at the entrance to the Place St Augustin were showing amber and that instead of putting his foot down on the accelerator in order to beat the red light, the idiot driver of a builder's lorry immediately ahead of him was braking hard.

He had little opportunity to feel aggrieved that the man should be behaving in a manner so extraordinarily out of keeping with his calling; it was all over in a split second. The immediate horizon grew dark as the back of the lorry loomed larger and larger. There was a jolt and his windscreen went milky-white.

For once, Pommes Frites wasn't wearing his seat belt. He gave vent to a howl of alarm and indignation as he rocketed forwards, rebounded from the dashboard as another vehicle collided with their rear bumper, then slid sideways across his master's lap.

Temporarily unable to extricate himself from the 50 or so kilos of dead weight jammed between his lap and the steering wheel, Monsieur Pamplemousse punched a hole in the windscreen and glared impotently at the tailboard of the lorry. As it swung shut a trickle of sand landed on his crumpled bonnet, adding insult to injury.

In the old days, as a member of the *Sûreté,* he would have thrown the book at the driver, going over the vehicle with a fine toothcomb in search of malfunctioning parts. One could be sure there would be many; faulty brake lights for a start – neither had emitted the faintest warning glimmer to signal the driver's intention. Tyres would have had their depth of tread minutely measured; although if the sound of sliding rubber on *pavé* was anything to go by it would have needed a micrometer to register any faint semblance of a pattern. Badly adjusted rear-view mirrors – and a quick nudge would have ensured they *were* badly adjusted – would not have gone unrecorded. Dirty number plates . . .

The traffic lights having completed their cycle, the lorry roared on its way. Monsieur Pamplemousse stared after it. The *salud* didn't even *have* a rear number plate!

He looked around for witnesses, but as though reading his thoughts, pedestrians on all sides were melting away like unseasonable snow on a warm pavement. Even the one-legged Father Christmas had disappeared. The only remaining person showing the remotest sign of interest was a man waving an admonitory finger at him from a shop doorway, as though accusing him of having been responsible for the accident in the first place. It was yet another reason for wishing he were still in the force. He would have taught the *imbécile* a thing or two. Dumb insolence . . . resisting arrest . . . running from the scene of a crime . . . the man would have been lucky to escape with a fine.

A loud blast from a horn somewhere immediately behind brought him back down to earth. The honking was followed by a shudder and the sound of tearing metal as the driver sought to extricate his vehicle by going into reverse. There was a loud clang as something metallic landed in the road. It looked like part of a wing.

Monsieur Pamplemousse adjusted his rear-view mirror, which had been knocked sideways by the impact. As he did so he gave a start, stifling the stream of imprecations he had been about to let rip with.

'C'est impossible!' He could hardly believe his eyes. Of all people! Had he been asked in advance to compile a short list of those he would have least wanted to witness his predicament, Monsieur Pamplemousse would, for differing reasons, have placed both names at the top.

What the Director and his wife were doing in the Boulevard Haussman at that time of day was anybody's guess. His boss normally drove in to the office from their country residence via the Bois de Boulogne.

Hastily converting the gesture he'd had in mind into the perfunctory raising of his hat, Monsieur Pamplemousse forced his lips into a smile which he realised must appear somewhat fixed.

As the large black Citroën DX25 drew alongside there was the faint purr of an electric motor and the window on the passenger's side slid open. The Director and his wife appeared to be engaged in animated conversation, but they broke off abruptly. Strains of soft music rather than words of sympathy emerged, floating on a waft of expensive perfume. Madame Chantal Leclercq was radiantly chic as ever; but it struck Monsieur Pamplemousse that the Director was looking a trifle edgy.

'*Monsieur, Madame.*' He sat back to allow his boss the privilege of making the first move.

'I hope this doesn't mean you are going to be late for the office, Pamplemousse!' boomed a familiar voice.

Monsieur Pamplemousse stifled the response which immediately sprang to mind, and tried to leaven his words with a touch of humour he was far from feeling.

'Fortunately, *Monsieur*, I was on my way to the garage. My *deux chevaux* is due for a service – the cocktail cabinet has developed a nasty rattle. It is, I believe, a fault common to the *marque*. On the other hand it may simply be all the empty bottles. Whatever the reason, it is as well to make sure . . .'

Catching a warning flicker from Chantal's limpid blue eyes, Monsieur Pamplemousse took a deep breath. 'I will be there as soon as possible, *Monsieur*.'

'Good. Good.' The Director reached for a mobile telephone and dialled a number. 'I will instruct my secretary to arrange for a breakdown truck to tow you to the nearest garage.'

'That is most kind of you, *Monsieur* . . .' began Monsieur Pamplemousse.

He broke off as Madame Leclercq, seizing the opportunity while her husband was otherwise engaged, reached out and rested her hand momentarily on his. It took him by surprise, causing a watery feeling in the pit of his stomach.

That Chantal felt it too was patently obvious, for she quickly withdrew her hand, but not before the gesture had left its mark.

Once again he was struck by the colour of her eyes; the colour, and as they widened in surprise, by some indefinable expression within. Anxiety? A cry for help?

She appeared to be on the verge of saying something, but it was too late. The Director had already finished his call.

'When you eventually reach the office, Pamplemousse, perhaps you would kindly contact Véronique with regard to the insurance. I have asked her to make sure she has all the necessary forms prepared.'

While he was talking the Director leant across in front of his wife and as he did so he, too, gave a start.

'I trust Pommes Frites is none the worse for the mishap. Would you like me to call a *vétérinaire*?'

Monsieur Pamplemousse glanced down. Pommes Frites was clearly milking the situation for all it was worth. Any passing insurance assessor catching sight of the injured expression on his face would undoubtedly have upped the potential damages on the spot.

'I think he is merely making a point, *Monsieur*. He probably thinks he is safer where he is for the time being.'

The Director looked relieved. 'You must bring him in to see me when you reach the office, Aristide. It is a long time since we had a get-together. I have forgotten. Does he prefer Evian or Badoit?'

'Evian, *Monsieur*. Bubbles make him sneeze.'

'Good.' The Director tempered relief at receiving a positive report on Pommes Frites' physical well-being with a steely gaze, as though everything he saw only confirmed his worst suspicions. 'I am pleased to hear it. I shall look forward to seeing you both later.'

The mellifluous sounds of the Blue Danube as interpreted by André Kostalanitz and his Hollywood Bowl orchestra faded as the window slid shut.

Finding his door jammed, Monsieur Pamplemousse eased himself out from under the steering wheel, climbed on to the seat and emerged through the open roof. In his wisdom, Monsieur André Citroën, the designer, had covered every eventuality.

He gazed after the Director's car as it purred on its way, driver and passenger once again engaged in animated conversation, almost as though nothing had happened. The price difference between the two vehicles was reflected in the damage they had

13

suffered. Monsieur Leclercq's DX25 had been barely scratched, whereas his own 2CV looked as though it was returning from a particularly riotous all-night party.

As the Director sailed through the lights, Madame Leclercq turned and waved back at him.

There were waves and there were waves. It seemed to Monsieur Pamplemousse that Chantal's wave was prompted by something more than a mere act of politeness. Once again he was conscious of a message being conveyed.

The image was still occupying his thoughts later that morning when he arrived, hot and tired, at *Le Guide*'s headquarters. Any hopes he might have entertained about slinking into the building unobserved were doomed to failure. Rambaud, the gatekeeper, couldn't wait to buttonhole him. Hardly had Monsieur Pamplemousse applied his magnetic card to the lock on the pedestrian entrance let into the main gates, than he was out of his hut like a shot from a gun.

'I know, I know,' said Monsieur Pamplemousse wearily. '*Monsieur le Directeur* wants to see me in his office.'

'And Pommes Frites,' said Rambaud, not wishing to be wholly deprived of his vicarious pleasure. 'Do not forget Pommes Frites.'

'And Pommes Frites,' repeated Monsieur Pamplemousse.

Concentrating his thoughts on what might lie ahead as he entered the building, he was conscious for the first time of warning bells. Pommes Frites was always made to feel welcome; there was nothing unusual in that. If you counted gift-wrapped bones, then Christmas brought him noticeably more in the way of presents than it did his master. However, joint invitations to the seventh floor were rare. Pommes Frites' presence on high was usually accepted with good grace rather than specifically sought.

Monsieur Pamplemousse's feeling of unease was reinforced a few minutes later when, having passed through an empty outer office, he entered the holy of holies and found the Director's secretary on her hands and knees in the middle of the room. A white napkin had been laid out on the carpet and she was in the act of emptying a large bottle of Evian water into a bowl; a little oasis in a sea of beige. All it lacked to complete the scene was a potted bonsai palm tree or two. Never one to query good fortune when it came his way, Pommes Frites set to with a will.

Bidding Monsieur Pamplemousse make himself comfortable in the visitor's armchair, the Director dismissed his secretary and then reached for a cut-glass decanter standing on his desk. Alongside it were two glasses and a solid silver paperweight fashioned in the form of *Le Guide*'s well-known symbol – two *escargots* rampant.

As he watched the pouring of a nameless

amber-coloured liquid, it struck Monsieur Pamplemousse that whether by accident or design, one glass was faring rather better than the other. Could it be an indication that for some reason as yet to be revealed, his boss had need of 'Dutch courage', or was he hoping the larger of the two would provide a mellowing effect on his guest? He hadn't long to wait for an answer to the riddle.

The Director held out the smaller of the two glasses for Monsieur Pamplemousse. 'This will do you good after your little fracas this morning, Aristide. It only goes to show one must exercise vigilance at all times.'

Taking the glass, Monsieur Pamplemousse raised it to his nose and hazarded a guess at a Marc de Bourgogne, that most potent of restoratives much beloved by those to whom refinement of taste is not the prime requirement. It was not one of the Director's customary tipples. He wondered if the fact had any significance. As a restorative it certainly did the trick. At the first sip he felt an immediate warm glow course through his veins.

Monsieur Pamplemousse eyed the glass reflectively. 'I was distracted by the sight of a *Papa Noël* in the Boulevard Haussmann, *Monsieur*. The poor man had only one leg and he seemed to be in a hurry. I had wondered about offering him a lift.'

'I daresay he was making haste for the same reason that Chantal and I left you as quickly as we did,' said the Director. 'There is a reason for everything in this world, Aristide. We were late for a fashion show heralding the forthcoming winter modes. The affair was in aid of charity. The handicapped of Lapland, I believe. Fortunately your lapse of concentration didn't delay us unduly.'

'I am relieved to hear it,' said Monsieur Pamplemousse dryly. 'My *deux chevaux* is, I fear, *hors de combat*.'

'A long job?' The Director made play with some papers on his desk.

Monsieur Pamplemousse shrugged. 'A week, *Monsieur* . . . possibly two. Apart from the shattered windscreen and the lights, there is a large dent in both the bonnet and the door on the driver's side. Also, one of the rear wings needs replacing. Since it went out of production parts are becoming harder to obtain.'

'Capital! Capital!' Dropping any pretence at a lack of interest in the subject, the Director rubbed his hands together.

Monsieur Pamplemousse stared at him. 'I am glad you think so, *Monsieur*.'

'Please do not misunderstand me, Aristide. It is simply that Fate moves in mysterious ways, its wonders to perform. As my wife was saying to me only this morning, it is almost as though certain happenings in life are pre-ordained.'

'That same thought has often crossed my mind, *Monsieur*.'

'Your misfortune, *par exemple*,' continued the Director, 'renders what I have to say singularly apposite.'

'I am glad someone is benefitting,' said Monsieur Pamplemousse coldly. 'It isn't every day one sees a one-legged *Papa Noël* in the Boulevard Haussmann. It would be comforting to know that it was pre-ordained and served some divine Christian purpose.'

'Since it put your car out of commission, Pamplemousse, the answer could well be yes. I have been thinking for some time that you look in need of a rest. All work and no play makes Jacques a very dull *homme*.'

Monsieur Pamplemousse relaxed. It was true that what with one thing and another he'd had his nose to the grindstone for some while now. He hadn't realised others had noticed it too.

'I suggest, Aristide, the time has come for you to take a holiday. At *Le Guide*'s expense, of course.'

'A *holiday, Monsieur*? At *Le Guide*'s expense?' Monsieur Pamplemousse stared at the Director. 'Won't Madame Grante in Accounts have something to say?'

The Director glanced nervously over his shoulder, then lowered his voice. 'For the moment, Aristide, this is strictly between ourselves. No one else, least of all Madame Grante, must know.

'However, before we go any further, I would like,

if I may, to digress a little and explain the way my mind is working.

'The other day I came across an article in a magazine on the subject of the *helix aspersa*. The humble snail, which, in many people's eyes the world over has, along with frogs' legs, always been a symbol of France. The article was based on a seminar the writer had attended in Czechoslovakia. It was short and to the point, and I have to say it made doleful reading.'

'My sympathies are with the author,' said Monsieur Pamplemousse. 'As an occasional contributor to the staff magazine I know these things are not always as easy as they sound. It is hard to picture what one could say at length about an *escargot*. They lead humdrum lives, dallying among the vine leaves. Innocents at large; blissfully unaware for most of the time of what is going on in the world, particularly when it comes to reading the minds of passing blackbirds . . .'

'They are also,' said the Director pointedly, 'and for much the same reason, becoming increasingly hard to find in their normal habitat. The Burgundian *escargots* – the *helix pomotia* – suffer from the modern use of insecticides; noxious chemicals thoughtlessly sprayed on the very leaves where they once made their home.

'In all probability, if you buy a tin of *escargots* in Dijon today and take the trouble to read the small print on the label you will find the contents come from places as far afield as Nagasaki and Smolensk. They bear little resemblance to the original incumbents of similar tins in days gone by.'

Monsieur Pamplemousse nodded his agreement. 'Only the other week Doucette saw some frozen snails in the delicatessen. They were labelled "Produce of Turkey". She refused to buy them, of course, but I fear she is fighting a losing battle.'

The Director gave a shudder. 'Mark my words, Pamplemousse, the day is not far distant when the label will read "Packed in Taiwan". You realise, of course, what all this means?'

'The good citizens of Dijon will have to promote other images on their labels, *Monsieur*, otherwise they will find the *Institut National de la Consommation* bearing down on them, levelling accusations of "passing off". *Escargots* with slant eyes, perhaps? Higher cheekbones befitting their Slavic origins? A fez adorning the heads of those in the illustration?'

The Director dismissed the suggestion with a gesture of impatience. 'That is not what I had in mind, Pamplemousse.'

Monsieur Pamplemousse essayed another attempt at solving the riddle.

'The pottery industry will feel the cold wind of change. Doucette's sister has a bedside lamp shaped like a giant snail. Its head lights up when you operate the switch. She is always grumbling because the horns cast a shadow over the pages when she is reading in bed. Souvenir shops will be going out of business . . .'

'There is good in all things,' said the Director. 'Try again, Aristide. You are getting warmer.'

Monsieur Pamplemousse considered the matter yet further. Clearly the Director had something very fundamental in mind. 'I believe that traditionally one of the local *Chevaliers du Tastevin* enjoy a one metre high ice cream in the shape of an *escargot* at their annual celebrations. As a symbol, that, too must be at risk.'

'*Exactement,* Pamplemousse! You have hit the snail on the head at last. *Symbols* are at risk.

'Now try transferring your thoughts to a venue nearer home.'

'*Merci, Monsieur.*' Deliberately misunderstanding the remark, Monsieur Pamplemousse glanced meaningly at the decanter. When the Director was in one of his guessing moods it needed all his powers of concentration; powers that could not be expected to perform unaided.

The Director obliged and at the same time put Monsieur Pamplemousse out of his misery. Reaching across his desk he picked up the paperweight.

'It means, Aristide, that our very own symbol, the company logo created nearly a century ago by our Founder, Monsieur Hippolyte Duval, which has adorned our publications and our stationery ever since, is also in danger.'

Pausing to let his words sink in, the Director glanced uneasily towards the wall at the far end of the room where the Founder's portrait in oils looked down on them. Following his gaze, it seemed to Monsieur Pamplemousse that the expression on Monsieur Duval's face, which in an uncanny way always seemed to act as a kind of conversational barometer, reflected disapproval of the present rather than any great hope for the future. He wondered if one of the cleaners had rotated the overhead strip light slightly so that the filament of the lamp cast a shadow. Whatever the reason, the Director must have noticed it too, for he quickly returned to the subject under discussion.

'I have been giving the matter a great deal of thought over the past few weeks,' he continued, 'and I have reached the sad conclusion that an effigy of two *escargots* rampant belongs to another age. What we need is something more forward looking . . .'

Monsieur Pamplemousse tried his best to be of help. 'Perhaps, *Monsieur*, you could turn one of them round so that they are both facing the same way – one behind the other?'

The Director shook his head. 'I cannot help feeling, Pamplemousse, that such a pose would give rise to ribald remarks on the part of some of our competitors. We live in an age where, given half a chance, people see evil in the least thing. The one bringing up the rear might well be accused of harbouring lascivious thoughts concerning his colleague. It would undoubtedly become a prey to graffiti and our image would suffer accordingly.'

'Evil is in the eye of the beholder, *Monsieur*,' said Monsieur Pamplemousse primly. 'In any case, being a hermaphrodite, the *escargot* does have the advantage of being able to keep its options open.'

The Director emitted a clucking noise. Clearly he had made up his mind and was not to be swayed. 'Dubious reasoning, Pamplemousse. There are many humans around today who lack such an advantage, but it does little to inhibit their mode of behaviour.'

Monsieur Pamplemousse ignored the interruption. 'It is an interesting fact,' he continued, warming to his theme, 'that many of the vines on which they graze are also hermaphroditic. They contain both the female and the male organs. When the anthers discharge their pollen, tiny grains of it are caught by the stigma which is situated at the top of the pistil. There they germinate and eventually reach the ovary where fertilisation takes place. It may just be a coincidence, but . . .'

The Director drummed impatiently. 'There are other factors to be considered, Pamplemousse. It is hard to picture, but I am told that since the advent of *nouvelle cuisine* some people are positively repelled by the thought of an old-fashioned *escargot* sizzling away in its shell on a bed of garlic butter. Before we know where we are we shall have massed groups of

23

animal rights protesters outside in the Esplanade des Invalides, baying for our blood.

'Political correctness is rife in the world. Already Michelin have decided to slim down their Monsieur Bibenbum. In Asia he is often likened to a sumo wrestler.

'What we need is a new logo; one more in keeping with present-day thinking. A logo which will in time become as well known and respected as its predecessor. A logo which will embody all the virtues, combined with an appreciation of the good things in life: integrity and steadfastness, alongside a love of food and wine. Alert and forward-looking, yet at the same time steeped in the past . . . like a modern *Curé* – neither fat nor thin, firm in his beliefs, yet open to the views of others.'

Monsieur Pamplemousse eyed his boss doubtfully. 'Such a figure will be hard to find, *Monsieur.*'

'I think not, Pamplemousse,' said the Director, fixing him with a penetrating stare. 'I think not.'

Rising to his feet he assumed his Napoleonic stance; one which he held in reserve for those occasions when he had some important pronouncement to make. It was also a pose which allowed him to address his audience whilst at the same time avoiding direct eye to eye contact. At that particular moment, for example, his gaze appeared to be fixed on Pommes Frites' water, and Monsieur Pamplemousse couldn't help but wonder if that, too, had been laced with

Marc. Pommes Frites had certainly lapped it up at record speed. Time would tell.

'It is my considered opinion,' said the Director at long last, 'that if the truth be known, when it comes to things rampant one need hardly look further than this office.'

Monsieur Pamplemousse gave a start. '*Monsieur*.' Instinctively, he drew himself up in his chair and tried out a few tentative Napoleonic poses himself; a Napoleon who showed mixed feelings, the recipient of a doubtful compliment from one of his peers.

'It is a signal honour, *Monsieur*. I hardly know what to say. When do you propose effecting the change?'

The Director came back down to earth.

'As soon as possible, Pamplemousse,' he said briskly. 'If we are to achieve it before publication of next year's guide there is much to be done. The advertising agency will need to be alerted in good time. Designs submitted for approval . . .'

He broke off. 'Are you alright, Pamplemousse?' he asked anxiously. 'You keep twitching.'

Monsieur Pamplemousse hesitated. 'I was wondering, *Monsieur*, do you see it as a silhouette? Black against white? Because if so, near my apartment, there are a number of artists in the Place de Tertre who do a roaring trade with their scissors during the tourist season . . . it might be possible for me to obtain a sample or two of their work . . .'

25

'That is one possibility,' agreed the Director. 'Then again, we could commission a well-known artist to paint a portrait. We might even, as they do with their labels at Château Mouton Rothschild, engage a new artist every year.'

'They could become collector's items,' said Monsieur Pamplemousse excitedly.

'Indeed. But at all times they need to promote the right image.' The Director took a quick slurp of his Marc. 'Which leads me on to the vexed question of weight.'

'Weight, *Monsieur*?' Having been indulging himself in a further flight of fancy during which he pictured Doucette dusting his likeness in oils on the wall of their apartment, Monsieur Pamplemoussse looked at his boss enquiringly.

'Weight, Pamplemousse,' said the Director. 'We must make the losing of weight number one priority. There is no time to be lost.'

'But, *Monsieur* . . .'

'But, nothing, Aristide. I realise it won't be easy; there will be a natural resistance to overcome. However, I am not talking of major surgery – simply a tidying-up operation. There will be no question of vacuuming away the excess layers of fat, as I believe is the current practice in Hollywood; simply a *soupçon* off here – a *soupçon* off there.'

Monsieur Pamplemousse hesitated. There was a certain lack of precision in the statement which bothered him, and while the chief was talking, his own mind began working overtime. He decided to take the plunge while he had the chance.

'I have been reading a book called *Je Mange Done Je Maigris, Monsieur* – "I Eat Therefore I get Thin". The author, a Monsieur Michel Montignac, explains how to lose weight painlessly using a new dietary system he has invented.

'He has abandoned the calorie theory, which he pronounces a myth, and instead concentrates the reader's mind on reducing his or her intake of the sort of food which embodies a high glucose content. According to his findings there is no limit to the amount you can eat provided you stick to his list of what goes with what.

'He has opened a restaurant where a typical meal might consist of poached egg and smoked salmon, followed by *boeuf Bourguignon* with whole-wheat pasta, then cheese and a glass of wine. I understand it is proving very popular. Customers queue to get in, and he has been forced to open several boutiques specialising in *foie gras* and chocolates in order to cope with the overflow.'

'I appreciate your enthusiasm, Pamplemousse,' said the Director sceptically. 'But are the patrons of his establishment any thinner when they finally emerge?'

'It is hard to say, *Monsieur,* without knowing what they were like before they went in.'

The Director waved impatiently. 'There is no time to test fanciful theories, Pamplemousse. Dietary miracles do not happen overnight. If we are to carry out the change before the next edition of *Le Guide* we must work quickly. Besides, I suspect *chiens* may not received a wholehearted welcome *chez* Montignac.'

'I'm sure Pommes Frites won't mind waiting outside, *Monsieur*. He has often had to on past occasions.'

The Director stared at him. 'That is a very callous suggestion if I may say so, Pamplemousse, and hardly practical in the circumstances.'

Monsieur Pamplemousse returned the gaze. There was really no anticipating the workings of the Director's mind. Who would have thought the possibility of man and hound having to part company for an hour or so would have weighed heavily on his conscience?

'I cannot help but feel a regime of biscuits and water once a day would work twice as well in half the time,' said the Director.

Monsieur Pamplemousse eyed him even more gloomily. 'I doubt if Madame Pamplemousse will approve.'

The Director lowered his voice again. 'There is no need for her to know, Aristide. Not if you carry out what I have in mind.'

Monsieur Pamplemousse raised his eyebrows. 'Which is?'

'I suggest you and Pommes Frites should take to the water for a week – escape from it all.'

'A sea voyage, *Monsieur*? I am unable to speak for Pommes Frites, but I fear I am a very poor sailor. I have never forgotten a crossing I once made of *La Manche*. I have no wish to repeat the experience . . .'

'That will not be necessary,' broke in the Director. 'What I have in mind is something much more tranquil. A voyage, Pamplemousse, on one of the great inland waterways of France.

'To the outside world you will be investigating the possibilities of waterborne *cuisine*. With that in mind I have booked you and Pommes Frites on a canal holiday in Burgundy. It will do you both good.'

While he was talking, the Director downed the rest of the Marc and rose to his feet. Keeping his distance from Pommes Frites, who had been giving the appearance of hanging on to his every word with more than a passing interest, he crossed to the door and made to open it. A clear sign that he regarded the meeting at an end.

'I wish you luck with the task in hand, Aristide,' he said pointedly. 'I realise it will not be easy, but you must be firm. Firm in making your wishes known and resolute in making absolutely certain they are carried out. I shall expect to see a big change when you return. I have made reservations on tomorrow's TGV to Dijon – the 8.05. Véronique will furnish you with the rest of the details. *Bonne chance!'*

The Director's hand felt unusually moist to the touch; the relief in his voice as he uttered his hasty goodbyes was only too apparent. It was almost as though he had been expecting trouble; trouble which hadn't materialised.

As the door closed behind him, Monsieur Pamplemousse looked enquiringly at Véronique. She opened a desk drawer.

'Some people have all the luck.'

'If that is what you call living on a barge for a week, condemned to a diet of bread and water,' said Monsieur Pamplemousse dryly. 'I have to say my cup of happiness is hardly in danger of running over.'

'*Allez raconter ça ailleurs à d'autres!* – tell that to the marines . . .' Before Véronique had a chance to elaborate, her telephone rang. She picked up the receiver and cupped it under her chin while she handed Monsieur Pamplemousse a large brown envelope with one hand and waved goodbye with the other.

'*Oui, Monsieur.*' She picked up a tray. 'At once, *Monsieur.*'

Monsieur Pamplemousse left her to it.

It wasn't until he reached the end of the corridor and was waiting for the lift that he opened the envelope and glanced idly through the contents. As he did so a frown came over his face.

The lift came and went.

Returning to the Director's office, Monsieur Pamplemousse found Véronique's room was once again empty and through an open door beyond her desk he saw she was busy clearing up the remains of Pommes Frites' water.

'*Monsieur . . .*'

'Yes, Pamplemousse . . .' The Director reached hastily for a pile of papers. 'I fear I have important work to do . . .'

'*Monsieur,* I have just been glancing at the brochure Véronique gave me, and all the way through it seems at first glance to place great emphasis on food and drink.'

'Everything in Burgundy has to do with food and drink, Pamplemousse,' said the Director impatiently. 'You should know that by now. Burgundians are pathologically incapable of writing the simplest sentence without introducing the topic. In schools all over the rest of France they teach children who are learning to read simple phrases such as "The man who opened the window is my uncle". In Burgundy it becomes "The man who is looking in the window of the butcher's shop is my uncle. He is a wine merchant specialising in Clos de Vougeot".'

'That being the case, *Monsieur,* would it not be sensible to avoid temptation altogether by following some other route? *Par exemple*, I believe there is a canal joining Paris to Strasbourg. For much of the way it goes through areas which are largely industrial . . .'

The Director exchanged a glance with Véronique, as though he could hardly believe his ears.

'The route you suggest,' continued Monsieur Pamplemousse, holding up the brochure to emphasise his words, 'seems to lay temptation upon temptation. If the illustrations are anything to go by, those taking it do little else but eat, drink and visit vineyards. The word "*gourmet*" appears no less than seven times in the first paragraph. On board, there is a guest chef from a two Stock Pot restaurant. In the evenings there are eight-course *dîners* accompanied by the finest wines. I really feel I cannot cope with it in the circumstances. One would be better off on a cycling holiday.'

'You can hardly expect Pommes Frites to ride a *bicyclette*, Pamplemousse,' said the Director severely. 'Present-day saddles are not designed to give a *chien* support where its need is greatest. No, he can run alongside the boat while you eat.'

'Run alongside the boat while I eat?' repeated Monsieur Pamplemousse slowly. 'He will not take kindly to that arrangement, *Monsieur*.'

'He will have to get used to it,' said the Director patiently. 'I am told there are a great many locks *en route*, so there will be time for him to rest while you are finishing your meal. There is no need for both of you to suffer.

'You are a good fellow, Aristide, and I can understand your concern. But you must be firm. It is the only way if Pommes Frites is to lose the necessary amount of weight in the time available.'

Monsieur Pamplemousse stared at him, wondering for the moment if he had heard aright. 'Would you mind repeating that, *Monsieur*?'

'I said, Aristide, that just because Pommes Frites has to lose weight, there is no reason in the world why you should suffer too. You must explain matters to him. Quietly and at length. I'm sure he will understand.

'To represent *Le Guide* is a heavy burden on his shoulders. Shoulders, Pamplemousse, that before the week is out must look as though the carrying of responsibility, rather than trying to support an excessive quantity of kilogrammes, is their prime function in life.'

Monsieur Pamplemousse glanced down while the Director was talking and as he did so he caught Pommes Frites' eye. There were times when he wished his friend and mentor were blessed with the power of language, and there were times when he was relieved he wasn't. It was definitely one of the latter occasions.

Not that Pommes Frites did badly with the limited vocabulary he had at his disposal. Coupled with his powers of sensitivity towards the reactions of others and his singular ability when it suited him to put two and two together in a remarkably short space of time, he often got the gist of things long before his human counterparts.

He had been giving the Director some rather pointed looks for quite a while. Now he seemed to be hanging on his every word.

Any feeling of disappointment Monsieur Pamplemousse might have harboured initially on his own behalf, soon gave way to one of pride on behalf of Pommes Frites; pride coupled with unease and apprehension at the mammoth task in hand. He wondered how he would break the news. It would be impossible to explain about the logo. Logos were not Pommes Frites' strong point. Along with most other Parisian *chiens*, he treated the doggy shapes painted at intervals along the *boulevards* by the City Council to indicate their preferred areas of defecation with a lack of recognition bordering on contempt. Nor would it be possible to demonstrate by example what was required of his friend; quite the reverse. Monsieur Pamplemousse sighed. He could see difficult times ahead.

Realising he was being addressed, he pulled himself together.

'I see there is a theatrical entertainment laid on tomorrow evening,' continued the Director as he scanned the brochure. 'A candlelit pageant in the vaults of one of the oldest firms of *négociants* in Beaune. By a strange coincidence the owner,

34

Madame Ambert, is a distant relation of Chantal – one of her many aunts. You may care to introduce yourself. I will warn her you will be coming.

'I might mention that she also owns a vineyard which is well worth a visit.'

Monsieur Pamplemousse felt tempted to say 'Only one?' The Director had married into relatives. His wife, Chantal, had them everywhere. Doubtless many of them boasted a vineyard or two. Loudier, doyen of all the Inspectors, having carried out some research into the subject, reckoned listing them all would fill a sizeable book. It was one of the factors that had led to Monsieur Leclercq's ownership of *Le Guide*.

'It is a delightful part of France,' said the Director. 'Chantal and I have stayed there many times. The hospitality is boundless.'

He returned to the brochure. 'The following evening Gay Lussac – an American wine correspondent of some renown – is giving a talk on how to avoid cellar gridlock caused by over-enthusiastic buying.'

'I cannot wait, *Monsieur*,' said Monsieur Pamplemousse dryly. 'That makes two pieces of good news in one day. To have the cocktail cabinet in my *deux chevaux* repaired is one thing, but to be told how to solve the problem of gridlock in my wine cupboard is an undreamed of bonus.'

The Director drained his glass. '*Au revoir,* Aristide,'

he said firmly. *'Au revoir,* and *bonne chance!'*

Monsieur Pamplemousse rose to his feet and signalled Pommes Frites to do likewise. 'There is nothing else you wish to tell me, *Monsieur?'* he enquired casually.

The Director paused. 'I think,' he said, 'that is all you need to know for the time being, Pamplemousse. Doubtless we shall be in touch.'

Had Monsieur Pamplemousse's thoughts not been concentrated on other matters, he might have registered a certain over-casualness about the last remark; over-casualness coupled with what others less closely involved might have construed as an indecent show of haste in saying goodbye.

Only Pommes Frites, his ears attuned to picking up any stray titbits that were going, registered the slight change in rhythm.

As they left the room he paused and looked back over his shoulder in order to make one final assessment of the situation. There was barely time to catch more than a passing glimpse before Véronique closed the door firmly in his face, but it was more than enough.

What with one thing and another, putting the various bits and pieces together and viewing them from all angles, it was Pommes Frites' considered opinion that the future looked distinctly unrosy, and it was in sombre mood that he joined his master by the lift.

The Director had been pouring himself another drink; one of the largest he had ever witnessed.

Earlier in the conversation there had been certain key words he hadn't liked the sound of at all; words like 'losing' and 'weight'. Add the two together and couple them with the look of relief on the face of Monsieur Leclercq as he collapsed into his chair and Pommes Frites felt more than justified in fearing the worst.

CHAPTER TWO

Monsieur Pamplemousse sat on the edge of the bed and took stock of his surroundings. Having resigned himself to nothing much more than a bunk in the way of sleeping accommodation, he was pleasantly surprised. Searching amongst his papers he found the brochure Véronique had given him.

For once, the text didn't exaggerate; rather the reverse. 'Once used for carrying petroleum, *Le Creuset* is a converted 38m x 5m working barge capable of carrying twenty-four passengers in style and comfort' hardly reached the heights to which most ad-men aspire, nor did it do it justice.

His own quarters – '*Vosne Romanée*' – was one of four double cabins named after local wine areas (the remaining eight were twin-bedded and *cru bourgeois*). It boasted a shower, toilet, washbasin, an open wardrobe and a dressing-table. The walls were lined with simulated oak matchboarding. The floor was covered with dark green carpet.

The floor plan showed the quarters for the crew were fore and aft.

On a dressing table beneath one of two portholes there was an ice-bucket containing half a bottle of Bricout champagne. Glancing up through a second porthole over the bedhead he could see a line of plane trees. Beyond their topmost branches a few wisps of cloud dotted the blue sky. The cabin must be partly below the waterline; standing on tiptoe to look out, the bank was level with his eyes.

The back of the cabin door was festooned with notices in various languages: *CHIENS INTERDIT*. PLEASE CONSERVE THE WATER. And what to do *EN CAS D'URGENCE* / *EMERGENCY* / *NOTFALL*. There was no lock. It reminded him of a seaside boarding house he'd once stayed in when he had first visited England after the war. All it lacked was a sign saying NO FOOD UNDER ANY CIRCUMSTANCES.

There the resemblance ended. The atmosphere aboard *Le Creuset* was informal to say the least. Everybody seemed to be on first-name terms, from Boniface, jack-of-all-trades and driver of the coach which had been awaiting his arrival at Dijon, to Sven, the *pilot,* a taciturn, pipe-smoking Swede who looked as though he had come with the boat and whose greeting, though warm enough, suggested he preferred his own company to that of others, much as Boniface had implied. What was the phrase he had used? 'Monsieur Sven, he runs a tight ship.' Sven's number two was an English *matelot* named Martin who was equally reserved; perhaps it had something to do with living on the water. Martin was married to Monique, who ran the bar. It was all very cosy, not to say incestuous.

Opening the champagne, Monsieur Pamplemousse poured himself a glass and took a long mouthful. It tasted crisp, clean and refreshing. There were biscuity overtones; an ideal *apéritif* wine. Recording the fact in his notebook, he refilled the glass, then lay back, allowing his mind to float freely as he adjusted to his new surroundings.

He had been looking forward to the journey down on the TGV, but ill luck in the computerised lottery of seat reservations had landed him with a paper rustler on the other side of the aisle. First the newspaper; every time the man turned a page – and there were a good many of them – it was a signal for a renewed and ferocious attack.

Then there had been paper-wrapped sandwiches, followed by a paper-wrapped apple of unbelievable crunchiness. That the man should own a black, thick leather executive type case with combination locks which sprang back with a sound like that of miniature pistols going off whenever they were operated had been a foregone conclusion. It was all done with a precision that had left him feeling distinctly twitchy. It was good to be heading for the country.

Boniface, the coach-driver, ran a tight ship too. Rope-soled shoes and a striped fisherman's jersey lent him a nautical air. White jeans set off his Mediterranean tan. Behind the wheel of the Mercedes coach he was in command; master of all he surveyed. He seemed to have a good line in aftershave as well. There had been a couple of girls with him at the *gare,* but they had melted away as soon as Monsieur Pamplemousse arrived.

Boniface was a mine of information. Even before they had left the station forecourt he had learnt all he needed to know about *Le Creuset* and what lay in store. A quick run-down on all the other passengers was thrown in for good measure. He had listened with only half an ear as the other ran through the list.

First there was a study group of twelve Americans from California. Most days they were scheduled either to go on visits to vineyards or to attend lectures.

Then there was an English wine merchant – a Colonel Massingham and his wife. A German couple – two men – '*comme ci, comme ça*'; Boniface clearly harboured doubts about their relationship, but they kept themselves to themselves. A Swedish lady travelling alone. An American businessman and his

42

bride . . . he owned a *journal* – a newspaper – and they were on their honeymoon . . .

At that point Monsieur Pamplemousse thought he had detected a slight hesitation, a change of tone, rather as though Boniface had been about to pass some comment, but the moment passed.

'Nineteen passengers in all; twenty now Monsieur Pamplemousse had arrived. It was not bad for the time of year. In August there wouldn't be room to move.'

It had been Boniface's considered opinion that he, Monsieur Pamplemousse, had done the right thing in joining the boat two days late. True, he had missed the opening 'welcome aboard' party, but the stretch of canal heading west from the port in the centre of Dijon to Fleury-sur-Ouche, where *Le Creuset* had tied up, was boring. The countryside was relatively flat and with the *autoroute* running alongside for much of the way . . . pouf! From Pont de Pany – which they would reach this afternoon – it was only another four kilometres – the scenery grew more beautiful by the day. *Bellissimo!*

Kissing his forefinger and thumb in the time-honoured Italian way, Boniface had gone on to demonstrate his command of other languages.

'Mind you,' eyeing Pommes Frites with a certain amount of alarm, he tested Monsieur Pamplemousse's knowledge of English while they waited at some traffic lights. 'Dogs are not allowed on the boat,

Monsieur. Did they not tell you when you booked?'

Monsieur Pamplemousse shook his head. 'The booking was done for me.'

'Ya?' Boniface had eyed him with respect, clearly hoping for more information on the subject, but Monsieur Pamplemousse had refused to be drawn.

'Sven is very strict on such matters,' continued Boniface, as the lights changed and they went on their way. *'Multo streng.'*

Not to be outdone in the language stakes, Monsieur Pamplemousse assured Boniface the matter was *pas de problème, non c'è problema,* nothing to worry about; Pommes Frites would be making his own arrangements. All the same, having said that, he had begun to feel more and more uneasy. His friend and mentor was transparently honest in all matters concerning his master; his loyalty unquestionable. He might be mortally offended when he learnt the truth.

It would be impossible to explain to him the reasons behind their trip and why he wasn't allowed on board. In that respect the news that dogs were *interdit* was to be welcomed. At least it would be possible to shift the blame. Pommes Frites was all too familiar with signs portraying a *chien* with a crossed line through it, although whether at the end of the day he would recognise his own logo on the front of *Le Guide* was another matter entirely.

'Do we have far to go?'

'Ten more minutes – maybe fifteen if the traffic is bad. Fortunately it is not the hour of *affluence*. We are moored twelve kilometres outside Dijon.'

'That is all?'

'*Monsieur* has a train to catch?' Boniface had looked hurt, as though a slur had been cast on captain and crew.

'We did not leave Dijon until Monday afternoon. It is a different way of life. It is not like the *autoroute*. Most days ten kilometres is maximum. On the straight *Le Creuset* has a speed of five or six kilometres an hour, but that is without counting the locks. Between Dijon port and where we are now there are seventeen locks. Another boat was ahead of us so there was a long wait at each. There is also the fact that the locks are closed between 12.00 and 13.00.'

Monsieur Pamplemousse had looked suitably rebuffed as he digested the information. 'Leisurely' – a word much bandied about in the brochure – sounded a fitting description for the days to come. Ten kilometres a day maximum was hardly likely to affect Pommes Frites' weight problem.

Reaching across for the ice bucket, he pulled it nearer to him, filled his glass with the remains of the champagne, then lay back again and closed his eyes. The slight movement of the boat and the sound of lapping water were making him feel drowsy.

Considering his fate, he fell to wondering why the Director had booked him on such an early train. According to Boniface most of the other passengers had gone off to explore the area on bicycles (Lapierre, with three speeds, dynamo and unisex frames). Others had gone for a walk, building up an appetite for lunch. The remaining few were taking it easy on the sun deck.

If Le *Creuset* was only going another four kilometres that day, he could easily have joined it in the afternoon and still left plenty of time for the evening visit to Beaune. A few kilometres wasn't going to make that much difference. Unless, of course, the chief didn't want to give him time to have second thoughts about the whole thing. He wouldn't have put it past him.

Turning their back on Dijon's hundred spires and steeply sloping roofs, its one-way streets, its mustard shops and its gingerbread, they swept under a railway bridge and turned into the avenue Albert 1er, joining the stream of traffic heading west out of the city.

Absorbing the passing scene, Monsieur Pamplemousse was reminded of Henry Miller's first reaction when he began his short sojourn in Dijon as a teacher. 'Stepping off the train I knew immediately that I had made a fatal mistake.' He wondered idly if he had too.

To the right lay the main railway line to Paris

and the north, on the left some Botanic Gardens he remembered being taken to as a boy. A huge psychiatric hospital came and went, then some pleasure grounds, in the centre of which was a large artificial lake. Beyond it he could see the Canal de Bourgogne.

Above the noise of the engine, Boniface's voice droned on. 'That is Lac Kir, it is named after Canon Kir who was mayor of Dijon for twenty-two years. *Cassis vin blanc* has always been the traditional Burgundian *apéritif,* but it was Canon Kir who made it popular by insisting it was always served at official functions. He was a man of the world – a Catholic, but also a communist. They do say you could fill the lake three times over with all the *apéritifs* that have since been made the world over.'

Monsieur Pamplemousse wondered if he could stand a week of Boniface's facts and figures, not to mention his driving.

Boniface had an unhappy habit of removing his hands from the steering wheel while he was talking, turning round to face his audience while making a point. He was at it again now, waving both arms in the air as he demonstrated the vastness of such a lake; the length and the breadth, not to mention the depth. It was one of those nonsensical statements you could neither prove nor disprove, and at that particular moment Monsieur Pamplemousse had no wish to attempt either.

They were now some way past the lake, travelling in the outside lane and about to turn left across the oncoming traffic. To his horror he saw an enormous lorry coming in the opposite direction. He tried to signal a warning to Boniface, but his hands felt heavy, as though they were made of lead. Bracing himself for the inevitable crash, Monsieur Pamplemousse sat bolt upright, pressing himself against the back of his seat, his eyes fixed on the road ahead. The other vehicle was now so close he could see the white face of the driver wrestling with his steering wheel. The roar of the engine grew louder and louder.

The crash when it came was something of an anticlimax; a mere tinkling of glass and a feeling of dampness. Over it all he could hear people screaming.

Removing the ice bucket and some pieces of broken glass from his chest, Monsieur Pamplemousse forced himself awake and looked at his watch.

'Sacrebleu! Eleven forty-five!' He must have been asleep for an hour and a half. Conscious of a throbbing in his head, he began rubbing it gently before realising it was the vibration of a diesel engine being transmitted through the bedhead. The pain, such as it was, must be the result of banging his head against the sharp edge of a reading lamp fixed to the wall. He looked out of the porthole. They were moored near a school and the playground was full of shrieking children.

As he lay back again he heard the sound of clinking glasses and snatches of conversation began to float through the open porthole. Drifting in and out of his semi-consciousness like so many dragonflies, they hovered for a second or two, before going on their way. It was a trick of the acoustics – or the wind.

'That guy been troubling you again, Hunn?'

He missed the reply as the *pilot* put the engine into full throttle to move the vessel away from the bank and into midstream.

'Tell him from me, I'll kill the bastard if he don't watch it.'

Monsieur Pamplemousse pricked up his ears, but once again the rest of the conversation was lost as they went under a bridge. By the time they came out the other side someone else – an English voice this time – was holding forth.

'The whole problem with fermentation in an area like Burgundy is temperature control . . .' The speaker sounded laid-back but authoritative. From the clipped tones, Monsieur Pamplemousse guessed it must be Colonel Massingham.

'Once upon a time the state of Burgundy reached all the way to Picardy and beyond . . . Luxembourg, half of Holland . . . The first vines were introduced at the time of the Roman conquest . . .'

Mrs Massingham's attention, if it were she who was being addressed, appeared to be elsewhere. She was probably used to being lectured.

'That bloodhound I saw earlier seems to be following us.'

Monsieur Pamplemousse climbed up on to his bed. Pommes Frites didn't seem too unhappy with his lot. His tail was up and his ears were back as he kept pace with *Le Creuset*.

'People shouldn't have a dog if they can't look after it.' Her husband dismissed the problem.

Monsieur Pamplemousse moved away from the porthole before Pommes Frites spotted him. He had no wish for the connection to be made just yet, especially after the last remark.

'I tell you, Hunn, there's a sun outage report this morning.' It was the American again. 'I heard it from a guy on another boat. He caught it on CNN. Come tomorrow it's going to be all-over grey.'

'I told you to insure, JayCee.' The girl sounded much younger. He detected a note of boredom in her voice.

'Boy, I got insurance on my insurance.'

'. . . the Canal de Bourgogne was opened to navigation in 1833 . . .'

Monsieur Pamplemousse set to work tidying up the mess left by the contents of the ice bucket. Fortunately the carpet was thick and most of the water had been absorbed. Only a few half-melted ice cubes remained.

Somewhere overhead a gong sounded and he heard a general shuffling of feet.

Removing the wet shirt, Monsieur Pamplemousse looked for something more suitable and settled on a green check. He lingered over the operation – the. dream had left him feeling strangely ill at ease – and by the time he reached the dining-room on the upper deck all the other passengers were seated. They eyed him with the proprietorial air of those who had assumed squatter's rights. He felt like a new boy late for school on the first day of term.

The décor was in much the same style as the cabins; light oak panelling on the walls, darker oak for the rustic style tables and chairs. There was a well-stocked bar at the head of the companionway. Doors at the stern opened onto the sun deck. Potted plants beneath the picture windows gave the feeling of being in a conservatory.

The party of Americans grouped around one long table were the first to break the ice. Greetings and names were exchanged; their brightly coloured open-necked shirts made Monsieur Pamplemousse regret he hadn't been more adventurous in his own packing. Reeboks were *de rigeur* in the way of footwear.

The German couple bowed stiffly, as did Colonel and Mrs Massingham. From their dress he could have picked them out easily in a crowd; the Germans in their leather shorts, Mrs Massingham, tall and willowy, in knitted twin set and pearls and a tweed skirt made of material which was almost identical to that of her husband's suit.

The four were sharing a table and Monsieur Pamplemousse had the impression that it was a less than happy arrangement. Colonel Massingham was holding forth on the subject of the importance of climate.

'. . . Bordeaux has weather, but Burgundy has extremes of weather. Intensely cold winters and often exceptionally hot summers with violent storms . . . hailstones as big as tennis balls . . . I'm not exaggerating . . .'

The Swedish lady was sitting alone at a table for two. She gave him a thin-lipped smile and then reached out and placed a red and white striped canvas bag firmly on the chair opposite her. The bag matched her shorts and could have been made from the same material. He was left with the choice of either sitting by himself at an empty table for two or sharing a larger table with the American couple he had heard talking earlier.

Monsieur Pamplemousse hesitated, then chose the latter.

'M'sieur, 'dame.'

The man didn't seem best pleased to see him. He appeared to be wrestling with some kind of report form, reading out loud and in the main answering his own questions as he ticked off a series of boxes. He barely acknowledged Monsieur Pamplemousse's presence. A half-empty bottle of Wild Turkey Bourbon stood within reach, but apart from an untouched basket of sliced *baguette,* there was no sign of any food.

'Fax?

'No.

'Telephone?

'No.

'Radio?

'No.

'Newspapers? Have you seen a newspaper, Hunn?'

The girl shook her head. 'Not since we left LA.'

'No.

'TV?

'No. What the hell do they expect you to do all day?'

'It was your idea, sweetie-pie.'

'Maybe I can hire a cellular some place?'

'You could try at the next village. You still haven't used the electronic translator I gave you.'

'It don't ask the right questions. Over three thousand questions and I haven't wanted to know the answer to one yet. I tried it in Dijon for your headache pills . . . remember? What did I get? Some kinda goddam capsules! I told the guy what he could do with them. You know what he did? He kept on nodding!'

Monsieur Pamplemousse began to wonder if he had made the right decision. It was too late to change.

The couple were both, in their different ways, larger than life.

The man looked vaguely familiar in a dated, old-movie kind of way. His shirt, carrying the slogan 'Hawaii Here I Come' and unbuttoned to the waist, made those being worn by his compatriots look positively sober. A heavy gold medallion dangled from his thick, bull-like neck as he leant over the table. Gold bangles adorned one wrist, a heavy gold Rolex the other. He had more hair on his chest than he did on his head.

Monsieur Pamplemousse racked his brains trying to think where he'd seen him before. It suddenly came to him. He was a cross between George Raft and Sidney Greenstreet with a tiny toupée. A clone of a clone.

The girl, on the other hand, was much easier to place. She was the nearest thing he had come across in real life to a Marilyn Monroe lookalike. Blonde and curvaceous beneath a loose fitting, white cotton dress. *Sablier* was the word – like an hourglass. Her curly blonde hair was cut short and her only jewellery apart from a gold wedding ring was a vast diamond encrusted engagement ring which could have doubled as a knuckle-duster. She was either very carefully made-up or she wore none at all. It was hard to say. He decided it must be the former, for her polished nails matched the colour of her lips. Even though she was seated, she looked as though she had left her engine running. It was probably permanently switched on. Glandier would have given her *doudons* a 150 watt rating. But then, his colleague Glandier, who had once been in electricity, compared all women's *doudons* to light bulbs. In his own life he had to make do with a forty-watter. Her eyes reminded him of the Director's wife, Chantal, and they were equally disturbing.

Monsieur Pamplemousse tried diverting his gaze towards a can of diet coke standing beside her, and when that didn't work he resumed studying the man again. It was easy to see why Boniface had hesitated when it came to describing them. They were an unlikely combination.

'Let me have a go.' The girl reached for the translator and laboriously typed in a sentence.

'Try this.' Glancing towards Monsieur Pamplemousse, she pushed it back across the table towards her companion.

The man pressed a button. *'Parlez-vous Anglais?'* A harsh, metallic voice issued from a loudspeaker.

For the briefest of moments Monsieur Pamplemousse was tempted to say *non,* but he decided it would be too restrictive to keep up the pretence for days on end. In any case, he felt himself melting under the girl's wide open gaze; he would have hesitated to use the word innocent, although innocence was the impression it conveyed. She had a voice to match; a kind of breathless wonderment.

Whether real or assumed, it produced the desired effect.

'A little,' he said, modestly.

'Jesus! It works!' The man stared at Monsieur Pamplemousse as though he had just witnessed a miracle. He handed the gadget back.

'Try something else, Hunn.'

Removing her gaze from Monsieur Pamplemousse, the girl typed out another phrase, then pressed the button.

'*Cette servez-vous,*' said a synthesised voice.

'*Cette servez-vous?*' repeated Monsieur Pamplemousse. '*Qu'est-ce que c'est servez-vous?*'

'Goddam! Now you've gone and broken it,' said the man crossly. He picked up the gadget and gave it a thump.

'Sweetie-pie, I was only trying to tell him lunch is self-service. You have to stand in line.'

'*Excusez-moi,*' broke in Monsieur Pamplemousse, 'I find the Japanese accent a little difficult, but thank you.'

'What is he?' growled the man, looking towards the girl. 'Some kind of Hercule Poirot?'

Monsieur Pamplemousse rose. 'I was,' he said. 'Some people would say I am still.' He couldn't resist it.

It was hard to say what the exact effect of his words was. Clearly the couple were taken aback; the man looked particularly grieved. Leaving them to digest the information, he turned towards a long table set against the wall behind him.

'If he's a detective how come he didn't see it was self-service?'

'Because he had his back to it, JayCee.'

Monsieur Pamplemousse had just finished helping himself to some slices of *jambon persillé* when he felt a presence beside him.

'Is that a "signature" dish?'

'*Comment?*'

The girl pointed to his plate. 'You know. Like a benchmark. The chef's special.'

'All over Bourgogne it is a "chef's special",' said Monsieur Pamplemousse. 'You take a ham which has been cooked in a *court-bouillon* made of bone-stock and white wine, with perhaps an onion spiked with a clove, some garlic and peppercorns, and of course a *bouquet garni*. Then it is chopped and compressed in a mixture of aspic and wine vinegar to which parsley has been added, and left to set in a cool place. It is delicious – a truly Burgundian dish.'

'I hate to think of all those calories. Is it vitamin enriched?'

'It doesn't need to be,' said Monsieur Pamplemousse, 'since none would have been removed in the first place.'

'Is that so? Ask a silly question! And these?' The girl leant over the table and pointed to some sliced eggs. Her dress was tight fitting around the hips and somehow managed to emphasise rather than conceal any movement within. With Glandier in mind, Monsieur Pamplemousse mentally upgraded her another 50 watts.

'Oeufs à la dijonnaise. It is another local speciality. You take some hard-boiled eggs and cut them in half lengthways. The yolks are then mixed with mustard, cream, chopped shallot and herbs, and returned to the white along with some butter and a few drops of vinegar, before being baked in an oven.'

Monsieur Pamplemousse gathered one in a serving spoon, dipped his finger into the centre, then placed a *soupçon* on the tip of his tongue. 'It is a test of the chef to know when to stop; mustard tends to lose its taste if it is cooked for too long.'

'Gee, that's some appetite you've got.'

Monsieur Pamplemousse, who had been about to cut himself a wedge of leek tart before moving on to other things, hastily changed his mind and applied himself instead to a large salad bowl. Lamb's lettuce predominated, but there was also some purple *roquette* mixed in with a sprinkling of endives and some other unidentifiable leaves thrown in for good measure. He helped himself sparingly, deciding to return later for what appeared to be pears poached in butter and sugar.

'There is a saying in this part of the world –

"Better a good meal than fine clothes". May I get you something?'

'No, thanks. I'm on a diet. We both are. I was just interested, that's all.'

Monsieur Pamplemousse gazed at her. He had yet to meet a woman who didn't wish to change the way she looked, but this was ridiculous.

'Hunn . . . You coming?' A warning shot was fired across their bows.

'See you. Have a nice day.' She disappeared as quickly as she had materialised.

Monsieur Pamplemousse followed slowly behind, placed his food on the table and made his way to the bar. He ran his eyes down the short wine list; some seven or eight red and an equal number of white. They were all from the region. Bordeaux might not have existed.

He ordered a bottle of red Pernand Ile des Vergelesses. Out of the comer of his eye he registered the fact that his table companions were about to leave. He wasn't sure whether to feel pleased or sorry.

The girl behind the bar held up a bottle. It bore the label of Domaine Chandon de Brialles. Her name, according to a badge pinned to her blouse, was Monique. She must be the *matelot*'s wife.

'Bye.'

As the couple squeezed past him, the man leading the way, Monsieur Pamplemousse felt a finger tracing a path lightly down his spine. It left him with an undeniably pleasurable tingling sensation.

'I will bring it to your table, *Monsieur.*'

'*Merci.*' Monsieur Pamplemousse wondered if anyone else had noticed the brief encounter. They surely must have; most eyes would have been on the girl, wondering, as he had, whether the dress was all she had on. He felt he could have answered the question with reasonable confidence.

As he returned to his table the Swedish lady left him in no doubt about her views on the subject. Everyone else apart from Mrs Massingham seemed to be intent on their food. Mrs Massingham had a faraway look in her eyes, but then, she probably always did. Colonel Massingham was extolling the virtues of double maceration to his neighbours.

The wine when it came had a soft, spicy quality. It hardly needed food. Still much too young, of course, but that was the way the world was going. Patience was becoming a rare quality. Patience and a growing awareness of the cost of storage space. Monsieur Pamplemousse reached for the notebook he always kept concealed beneath a fold in his right trouser leg.

As he began writing the room grew dark and he realised they were entering a lock. Martin materialised, waved to his wife, then disappeared up a ladder towards the top deck. A few moments later the gates behind them began to swing shut. That was followed by the sound of rushing water. The boat shifted slightly and then, almost imperceptibly at first, began to rise.

Monsieur Pamplemousse glanced around the room. As the sole representative of France amongst the passengers, he suddenly felt outnumbered in his own country. He hoped the others wouldn't want to play games in the evenings.

The room gradually grew light again and as it did so he became aware of a pair of eyes boring into him. Looking out of the window he saw Pommes Frites gazing down from the side of the lock. Raising his glass in greeting, Monsieur Pamplemousse toyed guiltily with the food for a moment or two, as though having difficulty in forcing it down. At the same time he looked for signs of premature malnutrition; the odd protruding bone, perhaps, or a tail at half mast, a dry nose even, but to his relief all seemed well. He shook himself. It was early days. Although it seemed much longer, he had only been on the boat a few hours. Give it time.

His conscience pricking him, Monsieur Pamplemousse pushed the plate to one side with a show of distaste. As he did so he felt a second pair of eyes watching from an open doorway leading to the galley.

Caught between the crossfire as it were, he nodded briefly to the chef and made a desultory stab in the direction of his plate. He managed to spear a

61

dandelion leaf, but it fell off the fork before reaching his mouth.

'You are unhappy with the food, *Monsieur*?'

'I am saving myself for this evening,' said Monsieur Pamplemousse.

The chef looked less convinced by the explanation than Pommes Frites would have done had he been able to overhear it. Pommes Frites regarded his master with some concern as the boat rose higher and higher in the water until they were almost on a level with each other and able to make eyeball to eyeball contact. What he saw did little to quell his feeling of unease.

In truth, until a few moments earlier he had been enjoying himself. One of his first priorities after their arrival had been to make friends with the kitchen staff, and on the strength of it he had dined early. Then there had been various run of the mill encounters along the way. If the proverbial red carpet had not exactly been laid out, bones and other titbits had been readily forthcoming. The *voyeur* in him had also been more than satisfied. It was surprising what goings on you could see from the bank. Had Pommes Frites been of a literary bent and able to put pen to paper, he could have garnered enough material for a sizeable tome.

Normally he would have been only too happy to share all these experiences, but in choosing to stay on board, for reasons best known to himself, his master was clearly opting for the monastic life; a life of frugality and self denial. A life totally out of keeping with his normal catholic mode of behaviour.

Pommes Frites gazed after *Le Creuset* as it nosed its way out of the lock. He couldn't remember ever seeing his master push a plate of half-eaten food away like that. Even if it wasn't up to scratch he usually managed to force some down in the interests of research. In the case of the *jambon persillé* it was unbelievable. Pommes Frites licked his lips in recollection. He had personally tasted the *jambon persillé* and he could vouch for its authenticity. It was no wonder the chef had looked upset. There was no doubt about it; something would have to be done.

Meanwhile on board *Le Creuset* Monsieur Pamplemousse gathered up his bottle of wine and a glass. Bereft of a plate, which had been silently removed by the waitress – a silence broken only by the pointed scraping of a fork against china as she deposited the remains in a waste bin – he made his way towards the lower deck with the avowed intention of drowning his sorrows.

He had almost reached his cabin when a door on the opposite side of the companionway opened and the American whose table he had already shared emerged and stood barring the way. He was swaying slightly and Monsieur Pamplemousse had little option but to stop.

'You going on the trip this evening?'

The question took him by surprise. 'To the *négociants* in Beaune? *Oui.*'

'And you're some kind of detective – right?'

Monsieur Pamplemousse nodded. It was easier than trying to explain his one time connection with the Paris *Sûreté.*

'I'd like you to keep an eye on my wife – OK?'

'It will be a pleasure,' said Monsieur Pamplemousse.

'Yeah? Well, make sure it don't become too much of a pleasure – right? You know what her problem is?'

Monsieur Pamplemousse decided not to hazard a guess, although he could have come up with a number of possibilities.

'Ever since she won the title Miss Goldenslopes, Napa Valley, guys have been ringing up wanting to tread her grapes. I'll kill any bastard who tries.'

'But do you not want to go on the tour?'

The question was brushed aside. 'I've only been on this goddammed boat two days and I've had it up to here with wine. That's all they talk about. I got other things to do. In the meantime she needs looking after – right?'

'If you say so,' replied Monsieur Pamplemousse.

'I do say so. She needs protecting from herself. You know what I mean?'

'I think so,' said Monsieur Pamplemousse with rather less conviction than before. It struck him that

Hunn might well need protecting from other people too.

'Like I said, I'll kill any bastard who thinks he can take on the job without my say-so. She means well, but she's too easy going. If she'd been born a chicken she'd have arrived with a "lay by" date stamped on her butt. You know what I mean?'

Monsieur Pamplemousse confined himself to a nod. It seemed the easiest way out.

'She's got this generous streak. So, like I say, she needs protecting from herself. She gets fantasies, right? Elevators, aeroplanes, the Golden Gate Bridge in rush hour . . .'

'You mean . . .'

'Yeah. Too right. That's exactly what I mean. So, watch it, OK.'

'I give you my word of honour,' said Monsieur Pamplemousse. 'As a Frenchman.'

'Yeah?' It sounded as though the promise rated rather less than an alpha plus. 'In particular watch out for the Bell Captain or whatever he calls himself. The guy who drives the bus. I don't trust him.'

'Boniface?'

'That's the one. He's up and down like a yo-yo. Either he plays with his dong or he's on the prowl. You get a load of his aftershave?'

Monsieur Pamplemousse was forced to admit the truth. It had been hard to escape the smell within the confines of the coach.

'I think it is Paco Rabanne.'

'You mean it was. He changes it six times a day.'

Almost as though on cue, a small door in the crew's quarters at the far end of the companionway swung open. There was a girlie calendar hanging on the back. Glancing towards it, they both caught a glimpse of Boniface making some last-minute adjustments to his person. Bereft of a steering wheel he looked smaller than Monsieur Pamplemousse remembered. He was having to stand on a box in order to see his reflection in a mirror.

Catching sight of his audience, Boniface hastily closed the door again, but not before they caught a waft of perfume. Patently, it was a different *marque* to the earlier one. He guessed at Eau Savage.

'What did I tell you?'

'Two down and four to go,' said Monsieur Pamplemousse.

The man stared at him for a moment, then his face cleared. 'Yeah. That's right. You know something? I like you.' He held out his hand. 'People know me by my initials – JC.'

Monsieur Pamplemousse hesitated before committing himself. He decided to stick to his surname for the time being. 'Pamplemousse.' Try as he might he couldn't bring himself to say 'AP'.

'OK. See you around, Pamplemousse. And don't forget what I said. No pompling around, right?'

As he closed the cabin door behind him, Monsieur

Pamplemousse reflected bitterly that he was hardly likely to. He wondered what he had let himself in for. Going over the conversation in his mind he wasn't aware that he had, at any given moment, agreed to anything, let alone acting as bodyguard to a nubile nymphet the like of which he hadn't encountered this side of the silver screen. One thing was certain, no one else in the wide world would believe his side of the story. He could picture the remarks some of his colleagues would make if they got to hear.

Pouring himself a glass of wine, Monsieur Pamplemousse spent the next few minutes slowly unpacking the rest of his belongings. Undoing the lid of *Le Guide*'s issue case, he removed the Leica and its supply of lenses and other accessories. It was time they had an airing.

He wondered if he should tell Doucette what had happened. It might be a wise precaution. There was no knowing who he might bump in to while he was away. He would have to concoct a suitably edited version, of course. It would need honing.

'Poor girl. She is clearly aware of her failings. It must be a dreadful cross to bear.'

Picturing Doucette's reply, he drank some of the wine. Was it his imagination, or had it acquired a certain acidity?

Someone struck up a tune on the piano in the bar; a rendering of Chopsticks followed by some passable boogie-woogie. An awful thought struck him. Would there be sing-songs after *dîner* in the evenings? Drinking songs from the two Germans; barber-shop from the group of Americans. If pushed, he might do his rendering of '*Sur le pont*'.

Hearing the tramping of feet overhead and the sound of bicycle bells he looked out of the porthole and realised *Le Creuset* was about to enter another lock. Once again there was darkness followed by a roar from the engine as Sven went into reverse thrust, holding the boat steady while Martin made fast.

The size of the boat was such that it left a bare four or five centimetres to spare on either side, hardly any more room fore and aft; it needed teamwork. This time, as they drew level with the top of the lock a gangplank was swung into place and he saw Boniface making his way along it, carrying a bicycle over his shoulder.

Mounting the machine, he headed off back down the towpath the way they had come. Presumably he was going to pick up the coach and drive to the next stopping point so that it would be ready and waiting in time for the evening excursion.

He heard the sound of laughter and more ringing of bells and looking out again he saw the party of Americans disembarking. Whooping with delight, like so many schoolboys let out to play, they spent several minutes circling around each other before heading off in different directions, some following the path Boniface had taken, others going further on up the canal. One of the members was already having trouble with his chain and had dismounted in order to do some running repairs. It reminded him of *Le Guide*'s annual get-together, when everyone let their hair down and shed a few years in the process.

An elderly weather-beaten woman in a blue smock who was operating the lock gates eyed the antics with stolid detachment. Her cocker spaniel regarded Pommes Frites circumspectly from the safety of a wired-in enclosure. Beyond it a few hens wandered aimlessly about, pecking at the ground. In the background he could see a line of some half a dozen rabbit hutches. A small patch of land to the right of a tiny cottage with a blue front door was filled with vegetables; potatoes, beans, carrots. A board fixed to a picket fence offered fruit for sale. Several gnomes and a small stone elephant with a hanging basket of flowers on either side completed the picture. It was a self-supporting, self-contained little world of its own.

He wasn't sure if he felt envious or not. It was a way of partially opting out of things without being entirely cut off. Winter would be crunch time. The huge pile of neatly sawn logs stacked near the kitchen door said it all.

Loading his camera with a reel of Kodak Panther

100 which he was trying out for Trigaux in the Art Department, Monsieur Pamplemousse swapped the standard lens for a wide-angle and went up on deck. To his relief it was empty. Trigaux reckoned Panther was the bees knees in colour saturation. Well, they would see. The sun was high enough in the sky to illuminate the rose-covered porch of the cottage, yet still provide plenty of interesting shadows over the water from trees on the opposite bank. He tried composing a picture with the lock-keeper's wife on one side of the frame and a bench with a solitary figure of a man reading a newspaper on the other.

He almost wished he'd left his standard lens on and loaded up with black and white. There were all the elements of a Cartier-Bresson; several in fact. The woman leaning against the lock gate, mistress of her domain, for a start; and in the second picture, the somewhat incongruous figure of the man dressed in city clothes sitting on the bench.

The only disturbing element in the latter would be the sight of Pommes Frites hovering in the background. He appeared to be munching a sandwich. From a distance it was impossible to tell whether it was cheese and tomato or plain ham, but whatever it was, he was certainly taking his time about it, oblivious to the complications he was causing his master.

Realising the boat was about to get under way,

Monsieur Pamplemousse took a quick picture of
the woman, then followed it with one of the man.
They could always be trimmed down later. The
man looked out of place; totally inharmonious, as
though expecting someone for a business meeting.
As *Le Creuset* moved slowly past, a black executive
bag came into view. Lowering his *journal,* the man
picked up a camera and pointed it towards the boat.
Instinctively, Monsieur Pamplemousse operated the
shutter for a third time. Of all unlikely people, it was
the paper rustler who had plagued him on the way
down!

CHAPTER THREE

Apart from Pommes Frites, who had taken it upon himself to establish squatters rights across the back seat, Monsieur Pamplemousse was the first to board the waiting coach after *Le Creuset* tied up at Velars-sur-Ouche. Master and hound eyed each other with a degree of circumspection, each trying to read the other's thoughts, neither wanting to be the first to break the ice. It struck Monsieur Pamplemousse that far from having lost weight, Pommes Frites might have gained a kilo or two, but possibly it was the way he was sitting.

Deciding to give him the benefit of the doubt, he turned to Boniface, freshly laundered and smelling of Xeryus. 'How far is Beaune?'

Boniface emitted a non-committal whistling sound. 'An hour, perhaps a little less. We are due to

73

reach the *négociants* at eighteen hundred. *Dîner* is at eighteen-thirty after a tour of the premises. The pageant is at twenty hundred.'

'How many kilometres is that?'

Boniface looked even less inclined to commit himself. 'Thirty-five . . . maybe a little more. It is hard to say. We go the back way – the route of the vines – and we stop from time to time.' He glanced at Monsieur Pamplemousse's camera. 'It is so that people can take photographs.'

Monsieur Pamplemousse hesitated. In his mind's eye he could hear the Director's voice.

'Nonsense, Pamplemousse. You heard what the driver said. The *autobus* stops from time to time *en route*. It is just what Pommes Frites needs. It will get rid of the cobwebs.'

Monsieur Pamplemousse made his way towards the rear of the coach and tested the water.

'Un promenade?'

A patently cobweb-free tail, which until that moment had been thumping the seat like a diffident upholsterer testing his workmanship after a difficult repair job, froze in mid air. Pommes Frites contemplated his master for several seconds as though wondering if he had heard aright, then settled matters very firmly by closing both eyes and pretending he was asleep. He'd had quite enough *promenades* for one day. Discretion being the better part of valour, Monsieur Pamplemousse decided

74

not to pursue the subject. In any case the other passengers were starting to arrive.

Colonel and Mrs Massingham glanced disapprovingly at Pommes Frites and pointedly seated themselves near the front of the coach; the party of Americans scattered themselves noisily around the middle section. The two Germans did their best to distance themselves from the Massinghams without making it appear too obvious, and the Swedish lady settled herself by the door, to the right of the driver's seat. Boniface looked as though he had been hoping for better things.

The girl was last to arrive. She had changed from her lunchtime outfit into a black crocheted dress; fashioned, it seemed to Monsieur Pamplemousse, by someone who had set out to make the largest number of holes out of the smallest possible amount of material. The task completed, the girl had been poured into it and no one had thought to say 'when'. The effect was all that must have been intended.

Holding a video camera above her head, she made her way down the centre of the coach. Envy and naked jealousy filled the air in equal parts, not least from Boniface, as she squeezed past Monsieur Pamplemousse and seated herself between him and the window. Her bare shoulders were tanned and smooth, the nape of her neck covered in a light down. It was easy to see why she had won the title of Miss Goldenslopes.

'Hi! JayCee tells me you're my bodyguard for the evening.'

Monsieur Pamplemousse made a gruff, but suitable assenting noise, conveying to those in front the minor role he had played in the decision, and that the guarding of heavenly bodies was an everyday occurrence in his daily round. He was keenly aware that the rest of the party was displaying more than a passing interest in what was going on behind them. Even Pommes Frites had gone so far as to open one eye a fraction. It looked a trifle jaundiced, as though he had seen it all before.

'That is my privilege.'

Relieving the girl of her camera bag, Monsieur Pamplemousse took her free hand and raised it halfway to his lips in a gesture of gallantry. It struck him that little further help would have been needed from him for it to have completed the rest of the journey of its own accord.

'The name is Pamplemousse.'

'You don't say?' She licked her lips. 'I had one of those for breakfast this morning.'

Monsieur Pamplemousse wasn't sure if the snort came from Mrs Massingham or the Swedish lady.

Boniface started the engine and attention was momentarily diverted as he carried out a U-turn. Having avoided backing into the canal by what seemed less than a hair's breadth, he drove through the village to the *autoroute,* headed east for some five kilometres, then came off it onto the D108, taking a short cut in order to bypass Dijon.

Dijon was dismissed by Boniface with a wave of the hand. 'The suburbs are now all built up. The only wine left is from Montre-Cul. You know why it is called Montre-Cul?'

There were no takers.

'Because the vineyards are on the side of the mountain and during grape-picking time people used to stop and admire the women's bottoms.'

Boniface's chuckle lasted all the way up the hill.

'And you?' asked Monsieur Pamplemousse. 'What should I call you?'

'I'm down as Gay Lussac, but that's just my pen name.'

'Gay Lussac?' Monsieur Pamplemousse gave a start.

'You've heard of me?'

'It is a very illustrious name in the world of wine. His work on the alcoholometer was invaluable.'

'Yeah, that's the one. I got it out of a book. Just liked the sound of it, I guess.'

'It was a good choice for a pen name,' said Monsieur Pamplemousse.

'My real name's Brittany – as in France, but people who know me call me Honey-bee.'

'I shall call you by the French equivalent,' said Monsieur Pamplemousse. '*Abeille*. Strictly speaking it should be *abeille domestique,* but if you will forgive my saying so, I do not think you are very domestic.'

'You can say that again. *Abeille*.' The girl rolled the word round her mouth several times. 'I guess I like that even better than Gay.'

'It suits you,' said Monsieur Pamplemousse. 'Once again, forgive my saying so, but neither do you look like any wine correspondent I have ever met.'

'So what's a wine correspondent supposed to look like?'

'They tend to show signs of their calling,' said Monsieur Pamplemousse. 'Too many invitations to too many tastings take their toll. The English are either elderly and very knowledgeable, or if they are young they are mostly products of one of their so-called public schools. They are like the *matelot*, Martin; they conceal their knowledge beneath a mask of schoolboy charm and a quiff of hair which falls down over their forehead. It is one of their great strengths. It disarms the opposition, who do not always take them seriously until it is too late.

'Your fellow countrymen are on the whole very earnest. They analyse everything to the nth degree and talk a lot about micro-climates, forgetting that in Burgundy every stone hides its own micro-climate.'

'And the French?'

'We French simply cannot believe that anyone knows more about the subject than we do. But that, I fear, applies to most things. It is in our nature.'

'So where do I fit in?'

Monsieur Pamplemousse felt sorely tempted to repeat that she was like no wine writer he had ever dreamt of. He modified it instead to 'You are like no one I have ever met before.' Spoken in a whisper, the effect was not quite as he had intended.

'Tell me more . . .' Abeille turned and fastened her eyes on his.

Monsieur Pamplemousse tried hard to consider them as objects in their own right, rather than as part and parcel of the whole. It wasn't easy. They were cornflower blue, bluer than they had any right to be, far bluer, he decided, than those of the Director's wife, and disconcertingly impossible to read; not so much expressionless as bottomless, without any kind of perceptible focal point.

'You are very hard to catalogue.'

That, too, came out not quite as he had meant it to sound, but once again Boniface saved the day. Selecting a cassette from one of several in a holder screwed to the dashboard, he slipped it into the player. After a short fanfare a commentator's voice began describing in various languages the route they were taking. At least it didn't have Japanese overtones.

The coach went quiet as everyone concentrated on the Route des Grands Crus: the Champs Elysées de Bourgogne.

Avoiding the main N74 heading south, Boniface turned on to the D122 running parallel to it. It took them along the bottom of the wood-capped slopes of the Côte d'Or, through the vineyards of Fixin and Gevrey-Chambertin.

At one point he slowed down to point out the vineyard belonging to the *négociants* in Beaune.

'. . . You are looking at Clos Ambert-Celeste. In France the word *clos* means a walled enclosure. It is a very old vineyard. Originally it was simply Clos d'Ambert. The word *celeste* was added at the end of the last century. *Celeste* means "heavenly". . . ' Bells rang in Monsieur Pamplemousse's head. The estate must belong to the Director's wife's family.

Negotiating the bends with one hand, Boniface pointed towards an imposing house set on the hillside away from the village itself, with its church and its cluster of tiny houses.

Clos de Vougeot came into view, then Morey St Denis. Absorbing the names on the signposts as they came and went was like reading from the roll call of a vinous hall of fame.

'Isn't it cute the way they name all their villages after the wine,' said Abeille.

Monsieur Pamplemousse gave her a sidelong glance. 'How long have you been a wine correspondent?' he asked.

'What time is it?' Abeille felt inside the camera bag and took out her translator. 'I'll let you in on a little secret. Not long – thanks to this. Name me a wine.'

Monsieur Pamplemousse thought for a moment. 'Since we are passing through Chambolle-Musigny, how about a Domaine George Roumier?'

He watched as she entered it on the keyboard. Half expecting her to ask him how to spell it, he was impressed when she got it right.

'What year?'

'Shall we say 1989?' It had been a near perfect vintage in the Côte d'Or.

She typed in the date.

'What is the name of the wine?'

'Les Amoureuses.' This time he helped with the spelling.

'Very good year. Ninety-five points. Fruity taste. Ready for drinking now.' Using the American style of classification, awarding points out of a hundred instead of the European twenty, the same Japanese voice issued from the tiny loudspeaker.

'Who needs books?' said Abeille. She snapped the gadget shut, replaced it in the camera bag, and began eyeing the passing countryside through the viewfinder of her camera.

Monsieur Pamplemousse sat back feeling deeply depressed. It was not what life ought to be all about. At this rate the day was not far distant when *Le Guide* in its present form would be made redundant and quite likely he would too.

'What did you do before you became a wine correspondent?' he asked at last.

Abeille switched off her camera. 'After I left high school I was in grunt and groan movies for a while before JayCee rescued me.'

'*Quest que c'est le* grunt and groan?'

Abeille licked her lips. 'You know the kind of thing. I guess you have them in France too . . .' Snuggling down, she kicked off her shoes, placed her feet on the back of the seat in front, and gave vent to a series of moans. They were accompanied by a certain amount of bodily writhing.

Heads turned. Monsieur Pamplemousse caught Boniface's eye in the mirror as the coach swerved and nearly didn't make Vosne Romanée.

'Geez! There go my Dolly Partons!' Abeille did some running repairs to an unsupported *doudon* which had become temporarily displaced. 'I guess I get carried away when I'm performing. I should never have let myself get talked in to having breast augmentation like I did.'

'How did you get to be one . . . a wine correspondent I mean?' asked Monsieur Pamplemousse, hastily changing the subject.

'It's what JayCee calls Kismet. JayCee's in communications. He owns a corporate presence in LA and he spotted me in reception one morning.'

'You were visiting him?'

'No, I was working there on the front desk. I'd just started and it was love at first sight. We were married within a week.'

'That sounds very quick.'

'JayCee's like me. He goes after what he wants and he doesn't rest until he gets it – one way or the other. I'm not the sort of girl to play around, so it had to be the other. After we were married JayCee made me wine correspondent for a newspaper he has an interest in. He thought it might stop me from getting bored.'

Very wise, thought Monsieur Pamplemousse. And it would mean he could keep an eye on you at the same time.

Once again he was conscious of the blue eyes fastened on him. 'So what business are you in? Aside from being an ex-dic.'

'I write about food.'

'You do?' Her eyes grew rounder still. 'So you know about wine too?'

'A little,' said Monsieur Pamplemousse modestly.

'Gee. Then you could help me with my lecture.'

'Lecture?' Monsieur Pamplemousse tried to remember what the Director had said about it.

'I'm supposed to be giving a talk on gridlock in the wine cellar. JayCee let me in for it. He says it'll keep my mind occupied. He didn't tell me I'd be giving it to a party of wine groupies.'

'It is not a problem I have ever encountered,' said Monsieur Pamplemousse dryly.

'If you live in LA you know all about gridlock,' said Abeille. 'It's part of the way of life. Like when it's time for laying-down do you prefer horizontal or vertical?'

Boniface turned the volume down a fraction.

'I take it as it comes,' said Monsieur Pamplemousse. 'There is no point in meeting trouble halfway.'

'Take it from me,' said Abeille, 'it's when you try and do it both ways at the same time the trouble starts. So will you give me a hand?'

'It is possible.' Monsieur Pamplemousse heard his voice answer from what seemed a long way away. The wine groupies exchanged disappointed glances.

'Gee, thank you. That's great. I've been lying awake thinking of it.' She planted a kiss on his forehead, then lowered her voice. 'Now I don't have to worry any more. All I know about wine is what JayCee tells me. He says you French put that bump in the bottom of the bottles . . .'

'Punt,' corrected Monsieur Pamplemousse. 'In English it is called punt. It is put there to collect the sediment.'

'Is that so? Well JayCee reckons it's a trick you French thought up to make it look like you're getting more than you really are.'

The coach slowed down and Monsieur Pamplemousse glanced out of the window as they drew up alongside a tall cross set against a low stone wall. The gently rising piece of land beyond it was covered in vines and the name of the vineyard was carved on a piece of stone let into a corner pillar.

'I think you should not say that too loudly,' he murmured in hushed tones. 'The owners would not take kindly to such a thought.'

Following on behind the others disembarking from the coach he glanced up. The air was crystal clear, but dark clouds were already gathering towards the west. It looked as though JayCee could be right about the weather. What was it Colonel Massingham had said? Hailstones as big as tennis balls. It would be bad news if Pommes Frites got caught out in a storm like that, especially if one landed on his head. Life wouldn't be worth living for a while.

A helicopter flew low overhead – probably getting in some quick crop spraying before the rain arrived.

He watched as it turned and zoomed in over a tiny patch of vines, the boundaries of which were marked by blue plastic bags tied to lines of upright posts. It was a simple way of ensuring the pilot got it right. In a region where each vineyard could belong to a dozen different owners, mistakes could be costly.

He shot off a couple of frames of film as the helicopter turned and flew in again. Then, using the wall with the name of the vineyard as foreground interest, he took a couple more shots of the hill immediately in front of them. It was a picture postcard view that must have been reproduced a million times, but one more wouldn't hurt.

Abeille rested her chin on his shoulder.

'Wouldn't it be a great place for having it away?' she whispered. 'Behind the wall.'

Monsieur Pamplemousse pulled himself free and stared at her aghast. 'That is hallowed *terroir* . . .' He made a rapid mental calculation, converting hectares into acres. 'It is four and a half acres of some of the most valuable land in the world.'

'You're just trying to turn me on,' said Abeille.

Mindful of JayCee's words of warning, Monsieur Pamplemousse took the girl firmly by the arm and led her back to the coach. The Golden Gate Bridge during the hour of *affluence* was one thing; Domaine de la Romanée Conti when the grapes were beginning to ripen was something else again. The thought of being discovered made his blood run cold. He would never live it down.

'I am supposed to be looking after you, remember?'

Abeille paused on the step and looked back at him. 'You didn't think I was being serious did you? With all these people around? Shame on you. What do you think I am?'

In truth Monsieur Pamplemousse didn't know what to think, but he knew one who would have been only too happy to oblige. Boniface was having trouble finding the right gear. In his excitement he put the engine into reverse and they narrowly missed colliding with an approaching tractor.

'Tell me about Beaune,' said Abeille, as they drove on their way.

'The place or the pageant?' Monsieur Pamplemousse was happy to change the subject.

'Whichever.'

'Beaune itself is a city which is almost entirely given over to wine; it is honeycombed with cellars. Most of the big *négociants* have their offices there. Then, of course, there is the Hospice. Each year, on the third Sunday in November, there is a great wine auction. It is in aid of charity, but it also dictates the price of wine for that vintage. It is part of *Les Trois Glorieuses* – the Three Glorious Days. On the Saturday there is a dinner at Clos de Vougeot. On Sunday it is the turn of the Hôtel Dieu in Beaune, and on Monday everyone repairs to the village of Meursault for lunch. To take in all three you need a strong constitution.

'Étienne-Jules Marey, who studied movement on film and effectively invented the movie camera, was born in Beaune. So was Gaspard Monge, who invented descriptive geometry . . .' Monsieur Pamplemousse broke off. If he wasn't careful it would sound as though he was echoing Boniface's cassette. 'It is also full of tourists. As for tonight's pageant, that is all about a character called "Vert-Vert".'

'Vert-Vert? Is that a he or a she?'

'Neither,' said Monsieur Pamplemousse. 'Vert-Vert was a parrot who lived in the fifteenth century. He belonged to some Visitandine nuns in a town called Nevers, and he became so famous that two centuries

87

after he died a teacher in a Jesuit college wrote a long poem about him. Generations of school children have had to learn it off by heart ever since. I had to when I was at school.

> *At Nevers, once, with the Visitandines,*
>
> *Lived a famous parrot, not so long ago.'*

'How did he get to be so famous?' said Abeille. 'Did he have a good agent or something?'

'On the contrary,' said Monsieur Pamplemousse. 'Vert-Vert lived a very pampered, sybaritic life. The nuns spoilt him, and instead of being adept at the usual phrases parrots learn he gradually became extremely fluent in ecclesiastical matters.

'News of his prowess spread far beyond the boundaries of Burgundy and one day some sister nuns at a convent in Nantes asked if he could go and stay with them for a while.

'At first the nuns at Nevers refused to let him go, but in the end they relented and he was sent off by boat.

'Unfortunately, during the journey down the Loire he met up with some Dragoons and that is when the trouble began.

> *For these dragoons were a godless lot,*
>
> *Who spoke the tongue of the lowest sot,*
>
> *. . . for curses and oaths he did not want*
>
> *And could out-swear a devil in a holy font.*

'By the time the boat reached Nantes the damage was done. Far from being enthralled by Vert-Vert's quotations from the Bible, the nuns were so scandalised by his foul language he was packed straight off home again in disgrace.

'Punishment was swift. For the indiscriminate use of oaths and for the embarrassment he had caused, the Nevers Council of Order condemned him to a period of fasting and solitude.'

'Oaths? You mean like swearing?'

'*Oui.*'

'Tell me some.'

'*Merde,*' said Monsieur Pamplemousse.

'And he had to go on solitary just because he said shit? Jesus – if that happened in America half the population would be shut away!'

'This was in 1493,' said Monsieur Pamplemousse. 'Besides, there were a lot of variations. There were other words.'

'Like what for example?'

Monsieur Pamplemousse racked his mind for some suitable examples. '*Con* and *lune* and *praline, par exemple.*' He immediately regretted his action.

'*Con* and *lune* . . . and what was the last one again – *praline*? I thought that was some kind of nut.'

Heads turned once again as Monsieur Pamplemousse tried desperately to think of a suitable translation . . . 'I am afraid my knowledge of English does not allow me,' he said at last. 'But it is something all ladies have.'

Disappointment manifested itself in certain areas of the coach.

'So what happened in the end?'

'Vert-Vert served his sentence and gradually the nuns relented.

> *Stuffed with sugar and mulled with wine,*
> *Vert-Vert, gorging a pile of sweets.*
> *Changed his rosy life for a coffin of pine.*

In short, he died of over-eating.'

'And we have to watch a pageant about it?'

'That is what it says in the itinerary.'

Abeille sat digesting the news for a moment or two. 'I was in a pageant once,' she said at last. 'When I was in sixth grade. Miss Screwpull of 1993. I was the one the judges most wanted to pluck at harvest time.'

'Times change,' said Monsieur Pamplemousse.

Signs saying *Visitez!* or *Dégustation gratuite* heralded the approach to Beaune.

The offices of L. Ambert et Frère – Négociants-Éléveurs occupied a large building standing a little way back from the perimeter road running round the outer wall of the city. There was little possibility of missing it; every half kilometre or so there were freshly painted signs advertising its presence. Other posters and hoardings drew attention to the pageant that evening.

They drove in through the open gates and crunched to a halt in a gravelled parking area alongside a row of cars and station wagons. Monsieur Pamplemousse gazed up at the signs. It wasn't quite what he had expected. During the briefing, the Director had mentioned nothing about there being a brother in the business. Perhaps he wasn't aware of it. The words 'et Frère' looked as though they were a recent addition; a hasty one at that, for the paint was of a different shade of white and they threw the original arrangement out of balance with the rest.

As they climbed out of the coach and formed a group near the main entrance to the building, an elderly woman he took to be Chantal's aunt, Madame Ambert, came forward to greet them and extend a brief welcome. Monsieur Pamplemousse had a feeling she was scanning the faces as though she might be looking for him, but before he had a chance to catch her attention she handed over to an underling and disappeared. Perhaps she had been frightened off by the presence of Abeille, who had slipped her arm proprietorially into his? Or else she had been forewarned to look for a dog. Rather to his relief, Pommes Frites had elected to stay in the coach for the time being. Guided tours were not his strong suit.

Boniface was already in deep conversation with a girl – a courier from a tour company.

Madame Ambert was clearly too well bred to let it show to all and sundry, but he got the feeling she was having to force herself into doing something which was total anathema to her; she looked distracted and unhappy as she left them to it.

They were each handed a tasting glass with the name of the company prominently engraved on the outside – he noted in passing that the words 'et Frère' were missing – and after a complimentary glass of an unidentified white wine they set off on an escorted tour of the eighteenth-century mansion house.

Ahead of them. Monsieur Pamplemousse could hear Colonel Massingham's voice droning on. The subject on this occasion was tasting glasses.

'. . . the shape is very important. The stem prevents the hand from warming the wine. The tulip shape is so that when the aromas are released they will concentrate at the narrow top. That is why, when tasting, you should never fill the glasses beyond the widest point . . .'

He wondered how Mrs Massingham stood it. Life with the colonel must be one long lecture. Perhaps, as mothers do with children, she had developed mental shutters, replying only when absolutely necessary.

On the pretext of studying the brochure they had been given on the way in, Monsieur Pamplemousse hung back a little until the voice was barely audible.

Originally the residence of a prominent member of the old Burgundian Parliament, the house had been many things in its time – including a hotel – before it had been acquired by the Ambert family, who had restored it to its former glory, furnishing it in the style of Louis XV.

Parts of it looked as though they were still lived in; the library, for example. Some of the bedrooms were also roped off to visitors and there were signs of occupation.

The vaulted rooms of the old kitchen and pantry area were festooned with artefacts of the wine trade. Ancient well-worn double shoulder baskets – made of willow and yoked in the middle – were now filled with bottles of wine for sale, the prices prominently displayed. Replicas of old cannons, once used for scaring birds, miniature dioramas of barrel-makers at work, glasses, corkscrews, grafting knives; everything had its price tag. Someone, somewhere, was making the most of things. The only item that remained unpriced was a gigantic wooden wine press housed in the former stables. It would need a crane to move it.

There was no denying times were hard. After a long run of good weather, two poor seasons coupled with the world-wide recession had caused prices to fall and many *vignerons* had been forced to add other strings to their bow. Who could blame the Director's aunt for joining their ranks? And yet, somehow, he couldn't rid himself of a feeling of disappointment.

A striking woman, genteelly handsome rather than beautiful, with a face which radiated toughness. Toughness, along with a stubborn streak. She would have had need of both qualities over the years. To be a successful woman *négociante* in an international trading area which until recent years had been almost entirely male dominated, couldn't have been easy.

Idly picking up a pair of pruning shears, Monsieur Pamplemousse turned them over. It was stamped MADE IN CHINA. At a guess the manufacturer's price must have been upped at least tenfold.

Displaying the tools of the trade with pride and charging admission was one thing; over-pricing cheap replicas was something else again.

Dinner was a pedestrian affair; a sad reflection of the festivities of *Les Trois Glorieuses*. It was taken at a candlelit table set in what must once have been the main room of the mansion. Ornamental mirrors lined the oak panelled walls. They were interspersed with unsigned monochrome paintings of unknown sitters, presumably past members of the family. The side tables were festooned with hand-painted china and porcelain ornaments. At least they didn't have price tags on them.

Perhaps not surprisingly, since it was billed as 'a gastronomic feast based on local specialities', the meal began with the ubiquitous *jambon persillé*. The ham was not a patch on the one which had been served at lunchtime. Manufactured rather than made with love and care. The pots of mustard on the table were not even from Dijon.

Monsieur Pamplemousse only toyed with the *boeuf Bourguignon* that followed. The wine came in large jugs and was too young for his liking. To say that it lacked 'body' was putting it mildly. It tasted as though it had been made by someone with a grudge against society; a product of one of Boniface's 'wine lakes'. Either someone was pulling a fast one or they had sadly underrated their visitors' taste buds. The serving girls, dressed in period costume, seemed hard put to raise a smile between them and gradually an air of gloom descended on the gathering.

Even the flowers were artificial and not very good at that. He watched as a fly settled on one of the blooms. It stayed there, clearly preferring the aroma of plastic to that of the food. He could hardly blame it.

At one point, as the meal was nearing its end, Monsieur Pamplemousse heard raised voices coming from a nearby room. Two men were engaged in a furious argument. It was conducted in French so most of it went over the heads of the other diners, but the venom behind it was all too apparent. One of the men spoke with an American accent and he appeared to be answering complaints about some aspect of the way that the place was being run. The quarrel was short and sharp, punctuated by the slamming of a door, which brought conversation around the table to a temporary halt.

Abeille turned to him. 'What was all that about?'

'I think it was a clash between the old and the new,' said Monsieur Pamplemousse. 'A debate between those who are resistant to change and those who are for it.'

Debate was putting it mildly. It had been a real slanging match. As they rose from the table and followed their guide down a stone stairway leading to the vaults, he decided the encounter had contained all the hallmarks of a bitter family quarrel; part of a continuing battle. A clash that had its roots in the dim and distant past.

The bulk of the audience was already seated. They looked cold, as well they might, for the atmosphere was damp and bone-chilling. A thermometer registered eleven degrees C. Abeille was going to regret her choice of dress before the evening was over.

The second row had been reserved for *Le Creuset*'s party and he found two places at the far end, near a lighting stand. At least when it came on it would give off a modicum of heat.

Judging from the batch of reserved empty seats in the middle of the row in front of them, local dignitaries and others of importance were expected.

As the audience sat waiting for the performance to begin, Monsieur Pamplemousse allowed his attention to wander. The vast stone-flagged, vaulted room they were in must have pre-dated the mansion itself by several centuries. Its walls looked as old as time – over six metres thick some of them, according to the guide.

Black drapes hung from the roof around the area where the performance was due to take place, but on either side he could see endless corridors lined with rows of bottles. It was like sitting on the hub of a giant wheel whose spokes radiated out in all directions; north, south, east, west and points in between.

The flooring in the corridors was of tightly packed gravel and the lighting came from candles burning in traditional wrought-iron holders. It made counting difficult, but at a guess the section nearest to them must have contained close on a thousand bottles; and that was only one stack. Multiply the total number by their market value . . . they were sitting in the middle of a small fortune. He would have given a lot to have tasted some of the older wines, rather than the mouthwash they had been served at dinner.

A hush descended on the audience as a small group led by Madame Ambert entered through a side door. She was closely followed by a man of about the same age. His face was bronzed and lined as though he had spent most of his life in the sun. Despite the chill, he was dressed in an open-neck shirt and thin plaid trousers. Several others followed, all men, presumably under-managers and other officials of the company.

Bringing up the rear was another older man. Monsieur Pamplemousse recognised him from a picture in the brochure. Fabrice Delamain, wine-maker to Clos Ambert-Celeste. He, too, had the appearance of someone who had spent much of his life in the open air. He looked ill at ease in his suit.

As soon as the new arrivals had settled themselves the house lights slowly dimmed until, apart from the candlelit corridors, the vaults were almost completely dark. Music issuing from loudspeakers hidden in various nooks and crannies filled the air.

Whoever was in charge of staging the production had obviously opted for working within pools of light, allowing the actors the freedom to appear and disappear as the script demanded, for as the pageant began a single overhead spot revealed a parrot on a raised perch. There was no sign of it being tethered in any way, and for a moment or two it was hard to tell whether or not it was real.

The opening music slowly segued into the sound of chanting as twelve hooded figures in white habits appeared from out of the shadows and moved in slow procession past the bird, paying their respects one after the other.

'*At Nevers, once, with the Visitandines . . .*'

Monsieur Pamplemousse closed his eyes as the familiar words brought back memories of his childhood. It was almost possible to picture the scene as it must have happened. And were the responses really being spoken by the parrot, or was it a theatrical trick? He opened one eye. It was impossible to tell from where he was sitting. The bird's beak was certainly moving and the shadow being cast on the floor grew and receded in turn as it shifted uneasily on its perch.

He was about to close his eyes again when he became aware of a movement nearby. At first he thought it was a rat, then he realised it was Pommes Frites arriving.

'Oooh!' Abeille gave a squeak. Luckily it coincided with the moment in the story when Vert-Vert set sail up the river Loire and the chanting of nuns gave way to a boisterous rendering of an ancient sea shanty, so it was lost in the general hubbub. Above it all there rose the voice of the narrator.

> *'For those dragoons were a godless lot,*
> *Who spoke the tongue of the lowest sots*
> *. . . Soon for curses and oaths he did not want*
> *And could out-swear a devil in a holy font.'*

Monsieur Pamplemousse reached down and felt a familiar wet nose. 'It is a sign of good health,' he whispered.

'Yeah? That's what they all say! Have you got a handkerchief I could borrow?' Taking advantage of the light on her right, Abeille wiped herself dry and set the video camera going.

The cast were barely halfway through the song when Monsieur Pamplemousse suddenly felt Pommes Frites' hackles rise. Ears cocked, body tense, muscles at the ready, he stared through a gap in the row in front. It was an all-too-familiar stance. Immediately put on the alert, Monsieur Pamplemousse concentrated his attention on the action, although for the life of him he could see nothing untoward.

The scene had changed to the quayside at Nantes where a group of nuns dressed in dark-grey habits anxiously awaited the arrival of the boat.

But it was not to be, for as the sound of cheering onlookers began to mount several things happened in quick succession.

At almost exactly the same instant as one of the nuns stepped forward with outstretched hands to greet Vert-Vert, Pommes Frites made a lunge – it could have been a fraction of a second earlier, or even a fraction later – but whichever way it was it took Monsieur Pamplemousse completely by surprise. Vert-Vert gave a loud squawk, fluttered into the air, and after hovering panic-stricken for what seemed like an eternity, plummeted to the floor, where he lay on his side, plainly no longer of this world.

It was all so unexpected the audience sat completely stunned and for a moment or two the actors looked equally thrown. Eventually Fabrice Delamain stepped forward and placed a large handkerchief over the corpse and everyone relaxed.

Bereft of its star, the cast manfully ad-libbed the second half of the poem. Extemporising much of it on the spur of the moment, intermingling past tense sadly with present, there were times when their performance bore all the signs of desperation, but at least the final lines were given an added poignancy.

> *'Stuffed with sugar and mulled with wine,*
> *Vert-Vert, gorging a pile of sweets,*
> *Changed his rosy life for a coffin of pine.'*

It struck Monsieur Pamplemousse as he joined in the applause that if someone had had the foresight to provide a small coffin the reception accorded the twelve thespians might have been warmer still. Even so, they took many more calls than they could possibly have bargained for. Relief, coupled with a desire on the part of the audience to get their circulation going again, added its quota.

He glanced down to see how Pommes Frites was reacting to it all, but he was nowhere to be seen. As the applause died away and the house lights came up, Monsieur Pamplemousse turned and looked idly back over the rest of the audience, hoping to catch sight of him. Those at the back were already making a quick getaway up a second flight of stairs which was being used as an additional exit. He caught a momentary glimpse of a familiar figure.

Could it be? Was it possible?

He would have sworn it was the man from the TGV again. One moment he was there, the next moment he had gone, swallowed up by the crowd.

'Hey! Look at that!' Abeille tugged at his arm. 'Would you believe it?'

'I know. I have already seen him.'

'No, I don't mean behind you,' Abeille tugged his arm again. 'Look . . . over there.'

Reluctantly, Monsieur Pamplemousse diverted his attention back towards the acting area. A stage hand dressed from head to foot in black – one of several responsible for moving the scenery during the performance – was holding aloft the handkerchief that had been used to cover Vert-Vert, a look of disbelief on his face.

'See what I mean?' exclaimed Abeille. 'Someone's made off with the goddam parrot!'

CHAPTER FOUR

The rain started to come down in the early hours of the morning. Monsieur Pamplemousse switched on the bedside light and checked the time by his Cupillard-Rième watch. It said three seventeen precisely. He had been wakened a few minutes earlier by a movement of the boat, then voices. It sounded as though Sven and Martin were attending to the moorings, but it was impossible to hear what they were saying above the noise of the wind.

After a while the sound died away. He lay back and closed his eyes, wondering where Pommes Frites was. Even though Pommes Frites had been the first to board the coach for the journey back – ready and waiting in fact – he had certainly been behaving very oddly, almost as though he had something to hide. There was no doubt in Monsieur

Pamplemousse's mind that he wouldn't be far away and that all would be revealed in due course. All the same, it would be good to see him sooner rather than later. At least it sounded as though the rain was coming down in sheets rather than lethal balls of ice; a plus of sorts.

Try as he might, he couldn't rid himself of the feeling that Pommes Frites had in some way been responsible, if not for the death, at least for the subsequent disappearance of Vert-Vert. It seemed too much of a coincidence for it to be otherwise.

According to the programme notes, the parrot had been on loan from a pet shop in Beaune, but he dismissed the thought that it might have made a miraculous recovery and flown back to base when no one was looking. Parrots didn't behave like homing pigeons. It was even less likely that in true thespian style it had been 'resting'; there was something very final about the way it had hit the ground.

It could have had something to do with the excitement, of course. It might have been a very old parrot, set in its ways, metaphorically speaking unused to seeing its name in lights. Did parrots suffer from stage fright? He had never heard of a parrot having a heart attack through exposure to applause. Rather the reverse – they enjoyed showing off. On the other hand, nothing in this world was for ever. Like everyone else, they had to die one day. Fortunately, the only person to witness Pommes

Frites' possible part in the affair had been Abeille, and she was hardly likely to say anything.

Abeille! Wondering if she was awake too, Monsieur Pamplemousse made the fatal mistake of deciding he would dwell on her for a minute or two before going back to sleep. The minute or two became four or five, then multiplied as he grew more and more restive. It had been a mistake taking a nap the previous afternoon; even more of a mistake to try picturing Abeille. Clothing her from head to foot in a nun's habit rather than the dress she had been wearing produced exactly the opposite effect to the one he had intended.

He tried thinking about the man on the train instead. That was a series of odd coincidences and no mistake. But then wasn't it often the case that you visited a strange town and then kept seeing the same person over and over again until you were almost tempted to greet them as old friends? Except that travelling around on a barge was hardly the same thing.

Sleep came to Monsieur Pamplemousse at last, but it was a fitful affair, and when he eventually came to nothing had changed. It was still pouring with rain, and there was still no sign of Pommes Frites. Neither was there any sign of the coach.

Having shaved and taken a leisurely shower, he toyed with the idea of wearing one of the open-necked shirts Doucette had packed for him. He decided against it. It was definitely suit weather.

He was in the middle of putting the final touches to his person when he heard the coach draw up outside. Glancing out through the porthole again he saw Boniface climbing out laden with *baguettes*. The rain had turned into a veritable deluge and he was having difficulty in staying upright on the slippery surface.

Making his way up on deck, Monsieur Pamplemousse found the dining saloon was empty. Everybody else must be having a lie in. He could hear someone hard at work in the kitchen with a bread slicer, and shortly afterwards a smell of burning toast drifted through a ventilator grill. The odour of freshly ground coffee followed soon afterwards.

While he was waiting he scanned the contents of some bookshelves in a corner of the room. It was a catholic selection; mostly French and English novels and guidebooks, with a scattering of German paperbacks. Probably they had all been left behind by previous guests. He skimmed through a visitors' book on top of the piano. It was full of complimentary remarks, along with the occasional drawing.

'Had a wonderful time! Can't wait for next year!'
'Weather and food couldn't have been better!'

He wondered what would be written at the end of the present trip.

Monique squelched into the saloon and placed a basket of toast on the serving table. She looked as though she had been out on deck. It was probably the only way to reach her quarters.

106

'Ooh, là, là!' She raised her eyes despairingly heavenwards.

It was the informed opinion of the crew that the bad weather would last for the rest of the day. Monsieur Pamplemousse would do well to find himself a good book; preferably a long one.

She returned a moment later with a pot of coffee, a jug of cold milk and a glass of fresh orange juice.

Monsieur Pamplemousse helped himself to some toast before turning his attention to the rest of the food on display. There were several dishes of *confiture;* raspberry, strawberry and plum. It looked home-made; full of whole fruit. Alongside the jam there were jars of honey, a plate of sliced Morvan ham, a large bowl of fresh fruit and a smaller one of yoghurt.

Some twenty or so minutes later, replete and at peace with the world, he removed his napkin and gave a deep sigh. It was a satisfactory start to the day.

He wondered if Pommes Frites had breakfasted as well. Knowing him, the answer was probably *oui*. Perhaps even now . . . He peered out through the rain-dappled window, but the towpath was empty in both directions.

Feeling at a loose end with no one to talk to, Monsieur Pamplemousse returned to his cabin. In his absence the bed had been made and the room cleaned. Ten out of ten for efficiency. A fresh-air fiend must have been at work, for the portholes had been opened and screwed back. At least it was warm rain and he was on the port side of the boat, sheltered from the prevailing wind.

Removing his jacket and shoes, he was about to make himself comfortable when there was a knock on the door.

'Hi!' Before he had time to answer, Abeille entered. She was dressed in a pink silk négligée which reached the floor, and she looked slightly the worse for wear, as though she hadn't long been up. Somewhat incongruously she was still clutching her video camera.

'Ssh.' She slipped in quickly, closed the door behind her, and put a finger to her lips. 'JayCee would kill you if he found me in here.'

It struck Monsieur Pamplemousse as a singularly unhappy opening to a conversation, but he didn't pass any comment for fear of sounding churlish. Why on earth the boatbuilders hadn't provided locks on the doors he couldn't think. It wasn't as though it had been built on the cheap. Perhaps they were obeying some obscure waterway regulation.

'I think I am able to take care of myself.'

'JayCee has connections . . . like Endsville.'

Monsieur Pamplemousse digested both the information and the tone in which it had been conveyed. 'In that case . . .' He began putting his shoes back on.

'Don't worry. He's the original couch potato. Anyway, he hit the bottle last night. He was in the bar when I left – he was still there when I got back. He'll be out cold for another hour at least . . . listen.'

Abeille held the door open a moment. Monsieur Pamplemousse heard what she meant. It was no wonder she looked as though she had spent a sleepless night.

Closing the door again, Abeille powered the camera and held it up so that he could see into the viewfinder.

'Hey . . .' She pressed the start button on the recorder. 'You're a detective. Take a look at that.'

Monsieur Pamplemousse peered at the tiny screen. All he could see was a curious montage of what appeared to be a number of white tree trunks intertwined with each other. The automatic focus had had its work cut out trying to follow the action. Much of the time the subject matter was too close for it to cope. Given the size of the picture and the absence of any kind of establishing shot it was hard to tell what was going on, let alone where.

'Is it a forest of some kind?'

Abeille snatched the camera back and took a look herself.

'Gee. Pardon me. I thought JayCee said he'd wiped it.' She flipped the recorder section into fast forward and waited several moments before trying again. 'That's better.' She pressed another button, then made a final check. 'Can I ask you a question?'

'Of course.' Monsieur Pamplemousse reached for the camera, but she held back.

'How many nuns were supposed to have taken part in last night's show?'

'Twelve, according to the programme.'

'Try counting.' She handed him the camera. 'I've put it on hold.'

Monsieur Pamplemousse raised the viewfinder to his right eye. This time the picture was of the pageant. The scene was a riverside quay in Nantes. It must have been recorded during the last few seconds before Vert-Vert met with his maker, for in the left of the picture the leading nun was in the act of stepping forward to greet him. Despite being on still frame, the definition was remarkably good. Video cameras were getting more sophisticated all the time. They could often see things denied the human eye. Certainly his own camera wouldn't have coped without first being loaded with a faster film. He hadn't used it for that reason. Even so, it was impossible to identify any of the nuns individually, for their faces were either in shadow or partly obscured by the hoods.

Starting from the left, there were . . . *un, deux, trois, quatre, cinq* . . . He paused when he got to twelve and tried again, this time taking it from the right.

'I make thirteen!'

'Watch this.' Abeille released the button, allowing

110

the tape to run on past the point where Vert-Vert disappeared out of the bottom of frame. Having zoomed in on the body, she had zoomed out and panned on to the group again. There were now only twelve.

'Isn't that kinda leery?'

Monsieur Pamplemousse looked at her curiously. 'What led you to spot it?'

'I was once in a live show called Snow White and the Seven Pervs. The guy running it was such a tightwad he made do with five. Two of the pervs doubled up. Ever since then I've always counted, I guess.'

It was a simple, if slightly bizarre explanation.

'Have you shown this to anyone else?'

She shook her head. 'Take a look at the parrot.'

Monsieur Pamplemousse ran the tape back a few frames to where Abeille had zoomed in on the parrot, then put it on to still frame again. Pressing the rubber cap to his eye to keep out the light, he checked the viewfinder focus with an external rotating sleeve, then took a closer look. There was a dark patch on the feathers just below the left wing. It didn't need the addition of colour to guess what it was.

'What do you reckon?'

Monsieur Pamplemousse considered the matter carefully before replying. It certainly put a whole different complexion on things.

'Who'd want to kill a parrot for godsake?' exclaimed Abeille.

'Somebody in animal rights?'

Abeille absorbed his words for a second or two. 'But if they were big in animal rights they wouldn't want to kill it,' she said at last.

Monsieur Pamplemousse wished he hadn't spoken. It had been a poor joke at best.

'Perhaps the bird just happened to be in the wrong place at the wrong time,' he suggested. 'It is a classic case of which came first – the chicken or the egg?'

'Meaning?'

'Meaning,' said Monsieur Pamplemousse, 'that something . . . either a movement from the actors, or the noise, or maybe even Pommes Frites, upset the parrot, causing it to fly up like it did. It is possible it simply got in the way of what was intended for someone else.'

He took another look in the viewfinder, but the figures in the foreground of the picture were merely vague, out-of-focus shapes. Had he and Abeille been sitting nearer the middle of the second row it might have been a different matter.

'May I keep the tape?'

'Feel free.'

'Is there any way of getting the picture blown up?'

'Only by plugging the camera into a TV.'

While Monsieur Pamplemousse was unloading the camera Abeille crossed to the porthole nearest the dressing table. 'There isn't a goddamned aerial in miles. What do people do all day? They can't go

112

out, that's for sure – not in this weather . . .' She broke off as her attention was caught by something further along the towpath.

'Hey! There's your dog! He looks wet through.'

'He will be all right,' said Monsieur Pamplemousse. He tried to keep the note of relief from his voice. 'Pommes Frites enjoys the rain.'

'How can you say that? That's like saying horses enjoy staying out in fields all winter. Who knows what they like except another horse? Don't you have an SPCA in France?'

'We have something similar,' said Monsieur Pamplemousse. 'At this very moment many thousands of its members will be getting wet through taking their pets out for a walk.

'Besides,' he pointed to the *CHIENS INTERDIT* notice on the back of the door. 'Dogs are not allowed.'

'So you're going to let him die of pneumonia? It's true what they say – the French don't give a damn about animals.'

Monsieur Pamplemousse stiffened. 'France happens to be a world leader in dog ownership. There is one dog for every six persons. It costs three times as much to visit a vet as it does to go to a doctor.'

'And that makes it good?'

'In Paris alone there are half a million dogs. They eat at the best restaurants. They have *caninettes* following them around clearing up where they have been. They have their own beauty parlours. They have everything except the vote and that is probably only a matter of time.'

'We're not in Paris,' said Abeille. 'And that's your dog out there and he's soaking wet. I know which way he'd vote if he had the chance. The party who give away free rain-hats. Look at him – have you ever seen such a miserable creature?'

Monsieur Pamplemousse's heart sank as he joined her at the porthole. Pommes Frites was a past master at the art of looking forlorn when he wished and he was certainly doing his best on this occasion.

At least the question of breakfast had been answered. He was holding something large and edible-looking in his mouth.

Abeille pressed herself against him and gave a shiver. 'You can't let him stay there. You can't.'

Monsieur Pamplemousse felt himself weakening. He caught the look in Pommes Frites' eyes as he drew level with the boat. It wasn't difficult in the circumstances since both were fastened on him. Soulful was the only word to describe them. The question of whether they were tearful or simply dripping wet from the rain was academic; the effect would have been the same either way.

Further along *Le Creuset*, Boniface was disembarking. Presumably having breakfasted, he was about to take the coach on to the next stopping point. Leaping on to the sodden turf lining the bank, he minced his way carefully towards the prow of the boat and began untying the mooring rope. The prevailing wind was keeping *Le Creuset* hard against the side of the canal and as Sven began building up the engine revs in order to move away, mud, churned up by the propeller, spread out across the canal. It was now or never.

Feeling in his trouser pocket, Monsieur Pamplemousse found the 'silent' dog whistle he kept for emergencies. He placed it to his lips and blew, hoping the note would be audible above the throbbing of the diesel.

An answer was not long in coming. Pommes Frites obeyed the call with alacrity. Sizing up the situation in an instant, he launched himself into space, executing an almost perfect docking operation just as Le *Creuset* began pulling away from the bank. Scrabbling for a foothold on the narrow outboard just above the waterline, his head and shoulders filled the porthole, effectively blocking off half the available light. The object he had been carrying in his mouth fell to the cabin floor where, for the moment, it lay unregarded.

Had he been present, the Director's worst fears would have been confirmed beyond doubt. Gaspard Monge, whose work on practical geometry had been commemorated by a statue in Beaune, would have put his finger on the cause of the problem straight away, possibly turning the situation to good account during one of his lectures.

Quite simply, it concerned the impossibility of passing a round body of a given circumference through a circular opening which happened to be some two or three centimetres smaller.

'Hey! That's terrible! You realise what's going to happen? He could be cut in half the first lock we go through.'

Clearly, the same thought had entered Pommes Frites' mind, for he began to struggle wildly, but he was fighting a losing battle. The more he fought to free himself the more tightly he became wedged. He was well and truly stuck, like a tapered bung hammered into the end of a barrel of wine.

Monsieur Pamplemousse made a half-hearted attempt to render assistance, but his heart wasn't in it, for something else had caught his attention.

'Hey, I've got an idea!' cried Abeille. 'You know what they say – what goes in must come out. You carry on pushing and I'll go outside and pull.'

The sheer nobility and self-sacrifice of the suggestion took Monsieur Pamplemousse by surprise, but she was gone before he could utter a word of protest. Who would have thought it? There was simply no telling with some people.

As the door closed behind her he bent down and picked up the object Pommes Frites had been carrying, placing it carefully on some folded towelling on top of his dressing table. A quick glance confirmed all that he had seen on the video. There was a small

mark on one side of the parrot where a slug had
entered. Hardly enough to have killed a human
being, unless whoever fired it had been blessed with
an exceptionally good aim, or exceptional luck; and if
it had been a serious attempt on someone's life they
could hardly have hoped for the latter. He sniffed
the area where the slug had entered, but it told him
nothing; the rain had seen to that.

Inasmuch as it was possible to look pleased, given
the unhappy situation he was in, Pommes Frites
looked pleased. In his view he had presented his
master with what was known in the trade as exhibit
'A'. He only hoped the fact would be realised in the
fullness of time, although for the moment he had his
doubts. Having covered the parrot with a fold of the
towel, his master was crouching down on the floor
with his head on one side as though he had been
taken suddenly ill.

The truth was, Monsieur Pamplemousse had just
caught sight of Abeille's upside-down face signalling
to him through the other porthole. She must be
kneeling down on the deck just above his head.
Communication was proving difficult.

'Prenez des précautions!' he called.

In the circumstances it was hard to tell if she was
giving him the thumbs up sign or a thumbs down,
but he assumed it was the former, for a moment
later Pommes Frites' eyes began to bulge.

In the event it proved to be one of those ideas

117

that are better in theory than in practice. All their combined efforts were to no avail. If anything, the more Abeille and Monsieur Pamplemousse pulled and pushed the less Pommes Frites showed any sign of being about to budge.

Monsieur Pamplemousse was still pushing at his end when Abeille returned. He looked up as she entered his cabin. She was soaked to the skin; the pink négligée moulded to her body as though liquid silk had been poured over her and left to set.

She gave a shiver. 'Can I use your shower?' Without waiting for a reply she wriggled out of the garment and handed it to Monsieur Pamplemousse. Other minimal pieces of silken material were added to the pile in quick succession.

A sudden and totally unexpected flash of lightning, followed almost immediately by a crash of thunder exploding immediately overhead, made all three jump. Pommes Frites registered alarm as the engine went into full throttle again and the boat began to gather speed. Sven was probably making for a clearer section of the canal, away from the overhanging trees.

They were barely under way when a door on the other side of the companionway was flung open and a loud voice called out. 'Hunn!'

'Jesus! JayCee! If he catches me in here . . .' Abeille didn't stay to elaborate. She made a dive for the switch controlling the shower light. As she disappeared into

118

the cubicle she pulled the transparent curtain across after her and turned on the water.

'Hunn . . . are you all right?' A series of bangs and crashes charted JayCee's progress down the corridor. There was the occasional response, but mostly the enquiry met with stunned silence. His voice grew louder again as he turned and started making his way back.

Monsieur Pamplemousse looked around wildly. The cabin, which at first sight had seemed a miracle of careful planning, now looked remarkably devoid of any of the basic requirements of modern living. Apart from the dressing table drawers, which he had filled with his own belongings, there was nowhere to hide a handkerchief, let alone a pile of sodden clothing. The bed was built-in. The wardrobe was what it had set out to be in the first place – a hanging space without a door.

In desperation he crammed the garments into the second porthole above his bed, then tried to close the brass cover. But it was fastened back to the wall by a complicated arrangement of wingnuts, so he drew a tiny curtain across instead.

Having plunged the cabin into semi-darkness, Monsieur Pamplemousse hastily began divesting himself of his own clothing; first his shirt, then his shoes and socks.

He wasn't a moment too soon. Following a peremptory knock, the door shot open and a cloud of cigar smoke entered.

'Anyone at home?'

'*Oui.*' Conscious of Abeille's silhouette on the transparent shower curtain, Monsieur Pamplemousse stepped forward and switched on the main overhead light. For the moment at least, it did the trick.

'I was about to take a shower,' he said reprovingly.

'Sorry, pal. You been in here all the time?'

'Since I took *petit déjeuner* . . .' Monsieur Pamplemousse broke off. 'There is something wrong?'

'How come you got a trophy on the wall?' demanded JayCee.

Monsieur Pamplemousse followed the other's gaze. Mercifully Pommes Frites, having just been struck by an overhanging branch, was wearing his glazed expression. Apart from a drip on the end of his nose his head had mostly dried out.

'You do not have one of those?' asked Monsieur Pamplemousse innocently.

'I booked the Beaune suite and all I got is pictures of goddammed wine bottles,' said JayCee. 'A lot of crap about vintages. Don't you guys have vintage enhancers over here? All you do is dial the year you want, switch on and wait while it ionizes the molecules or some goddammed thing. Ask Hunn. She knows. She got me one for Thanksgiving.'

Crossing to take a closer look, he poked the end of Pommes Frites' nose. The drip came away on his finger.

'I guess I've seen everything now. Lions, elks,

120

deer, bears. I even knew a guy once had a crocodile. Used to bang his head on it every time he went to poke the fire . . . but a dog!'

Monsieur Pamplemousse hastily removed his trousers and hung them over Pommes Frites' head.

'They do wonderful things these days,' he said, adding his hat for good measure.

JayCee frowned. 'Hey! I can find a better use for it than that. How about doing a deal for a couple of my wine bottles?'

'There has been a slight accident,' said Monsieur Pamplemousse desperately. 'They are coming to remount it at any moment. In the meantime, I have promised to look after it.'

'You call that looking after it? There's only one thing you're supposed to be looking after,' said JayCee meaningly. 'We had an arrangement. Remember?'

'Pardon?'

'Hunn.' JayCee pointed his cigar at Monsieur Pamplemousse.

'You merely asked me to accompany her to the pageant last night,' said Monsieur Pamplemousse. 'I carried out your wishes and saw her safely back.'

'Yeah, well, she ain't around now. From now on you got a full-time job. If Hunn goes missing she's your responsibility. And it starts right here as of this moment. Right?'

Monsieur Pamplemousse hesitated, torn between a desire to absolve himself of responsibility for

Abeille's well-being and a need to get rid of JayCee with all possible speed.

'It is possible she may have gone for a walk,' he said lamely.

'In this weather? Have you seen what it's like outside? Anyway, we're not talking Marco Polo, right? Hunn don't like walking anywhere. She gets more pleasure staying right where she is and lying on her butt, you understand what I'm saying?'

Monsieur Pamplemousse nodded unhappily.

'Am I right or am I wrong?'

'I am sure you are right,' said Monsieur Pamplemousse. He doubted if JayCee had ever considered the possibility that he might be wrong.

'I suggest you start with that Boniface character.'

Monsieur Pamplemousse clutched at the passing straw. 'Ah, now there I can help. I saw him go off in the coach after breakfast.'

'Alone?'

'Alone,' said Monsieur Pamplemousse.

'Yeah, well that's something.' JayCee sounded mollified.

He took one last look round the cabin. As he did so there was a muffled sneeze.

JayCee turned. 'Hey! You'd better take your shower. Don't let me stop you.'

Recovering his trousers from where they had fallen, Monsieur Pamplemousse replaced them on

Pommes Frites, then made for the shower. As he entered he took the precaution of turning off the light. The water beneath the overhead jets was warm and soothing, but as was so often the case, it only emphasised the coldness without. He moved further in. Abeille's body felt warm and firm.

'I tell you something – if I catch anyone playing around with Hunn I'll kill the bastard.' JayCee raised his voice so that all the ship could hear and take due warning.

'I am sure it is nothing like that,' called Monsieur Pamplemousse. 'There is doubtless a very simple explanation. Besides, it is a matter of trust . . .'

'Trust?' bellowed JayCee. 'What the hell's trust got to do with it? A guy that don't protect his own property deserves what he gets, right?'

'Right!' echoed Monsieur Pamplemousse unhappily.

'Hey, that's rude!' hissed Abeille in his ear. 'If you come any closer I shall scream.'

Monsieur Pamplemousse jumped back as though he had been shot. Given that only a moment before Abeille had been lathering areas of his own property which, to carry JayCee's simile a stage further, would normally have been marked *PROPRIETÉ PRIVÉ,* he felt very hard done by.

'Slowly,' said JayCee. 'Like there was no tomorrow. You know what I mean?'

It struck Monsieur Pamplemousse that in another life JayCee would make a very good parrot.

'Please don't turn off the main light when you go,' he called.

As the door closed behind JayCee, Abeille let out a sigh of relief.

'Wasn't that the most turning-on thing ever?' she breathed.

'*Non*,' said Monsieur Pamplemousse with conviction. '*Ça n'est pas une* "turn-on"!'

'You could have fooled me,' said Abeille. 'Have you felt your molecules lately?'

Hastily disengaging himself in case she decided to argue the point, Monsieur Pamplemousse made good his escape and began drying himself briskly with the remaining towel. Pommes Frites, who had already managed to shake himself free again from his master's trousers, watched gloomily from the porthole as Abeille emerged from the shower.

She looked around. 'So, what have you done with them?'

'Them?' Monsieur Pamplemousse looked at her blankly for a moment before he realised what she meant. He glanced towards the drawn curtains, then sought refuge behind the towel again, dutifully turning his back as Abeille crossed to the porthole and drew the curtain.

'Oh, my!'

Hearing a gasp he turned and saw Abeille gazing back at him with a finger in her mouth, the picture of innocence.

'Silly me! I guess my hand must have slipped.'

'*Sacrebleu!*'

Climbing on to the bed, Monsieur Pamplemousse poked his head out through the porthole as far as it would go.

'*C'est impossible!*'

They were passing slowly through a wooded section of the canal and Abeille's garments were clearly visible some twenty or thirty metres away, impaled on the branches of an overhanging tree, like someone's washing hanging out to dry or, in this case, get wetter still.

'*Nom d'un nom!*'

Abeille paused in her drying. 'Are you trying to tell me something?' she asked.

'I am afraid,' said Monsieur Pamplemousse, 'your négligée is lost beyond recall.'

'I can recall it,' said Abeille firmly. 'So will JayCee. It's Arnold Scaasi and he picked up the bill!'

Tossing the towel to one side, she climbed onto the bed. 'You'll just have to get hold of something to replace it, won't you?'

Monsieur Pamplemousse gazed gloomily out of the porthole. Outward signs of civilisation in any shape or form were conspicuous by their absence. Neither Yves St Laurent, nor any of his colleagues in the rue Matignon, had seen fit to open up a boutique on the banks of the Canal de Bourgogne, and he could hardly blame them. Trade would not be brisk at any time of the year.

'You may have to wait a little while,' he said.

'I'm not going any place.' Abeille lay back and adopted a cycling on the back position. 'How about you?'

Monsieur Pamplemousse stared at her and then at Pommes Frites. Clutching his forehead, he realised his hand was trembling. Dressing as quickly as possible, he placed himself strategically between the bed and the door.

'If you mean what I think you mean, I'm afraid that is not possible.'

'Not possible?' Abeille free-wheeled for a moment.

'I have given my word,' said Monsieur Pamplemousse.

'You've done what?'

'I have given my word,' said Monsieur Pamplemousse virtuously. 'As a Frenchman.'

Abeille lay back and began pedalling again. 'That's all right, then. *Pas de problème* as you folks over here say.'

'You do not understand. I do not wish to sound like a lecturer, but . . .'

'What time is it?'

Monsieur Pamplemousse looked at his watch. 'It is almost ten o'clock.' Had anyone suggested to him over breakfast that before an hour had passed he would find himself caught between a bloodhound stuck in a porthole and a naked female doing her *bicyclette* exercises on his bed, he would have laughed in their face.

126

Abeille sat bolt upright. 'Jesus, the lecture! I forgot to tell you. They've brought it forward to this morning because of the weather. I saw a notice on the way up.'

Busy with his own thoughts, Monsieur Pamplemousse absorbed the information without totally registering the implications.

'Will you be giving it in the lounge,' asked Abeille, taking up her cycling position again, 'or shall we invite them all down here?'

Monsieur Pamplemousse turned to the wardrobe. 'You are welcome to borrow one of my suits.'

'And have JayCee catch me in it?'

It was a compelling argument.

'I will be back as soon as I possibly can,' said Monsieur Pamplemousse unhappily. 'Right?'

'Right!' Abeille resumed her pedalling. 'Have a nice day!'

CHAPTER FIVE

'Hands up,' said Monsieur Pamplemousse, 'all those who suffer from gridlock problems in their cellar.'

Twelve hands shot up. Colonel Massingham bestowed on him a look of contempt. There was one in every class.

'Badly?' enquired Monsieur Pamplemousse of the others.

'Like there was no tomorrow,' said one of their number.

'I have my pre-phyloxera Bordeaux mixed in with my '85s.' The speaker looked as though he couldn't be more than thirty. It was always sobering when tragedy struck the young.

Monsieur Pamplemousse waited patiently while unfamiliar phrases like 'capacity management', 'distressed produce' and 'non-viable situation' were bandied about.

He gazed out of the window in search of inspiration. The sycamore trees lining the banks of the Canal de Bourgogne were laden with mistletoe. It looked as though Burgundy might be in for a hard winter. Early frosts following hard on the rain would be bad news; a repeat of the three weeks of torrential rain and hailstorms in the summer of '83 which had caused widespread rot. Beyond the trees, lights from a solitary house stood out like a beacon in the gloom. A torrent of brown water raced past the house down a narrow lane, disgorging into a drainage ditch running parallel to the canal. Further along the bank a man in oilskins was attending to a flood gate. A small cabin cruiser went slowly past in the opposite direction. The man at the wheel waved. Small white faces were pressed against the cabin windows.

Pencils poised, his audience awaited the pearls of wisdom for which, he reflected, they had doubtless paid good money.

'I can tell you a worse problem,' said Monsieur Pamplemousse. 'In all the villages and towns around here everyone has their own private store of wine. If this rain keeps on their cellars will, in time, become flooded.'

Almost beginning to enjoy himself, he pointed to a man in the back row.

'What happens then?'

'Sir, I guess they'll have to man the pumps – get going with the squeegees and start mopping up.'

'They could call out the fire brigade,' suggested another.

'Sir. How about holding underwater parties?'

Monsieur Pamplemousse waited for the hubbub to die down as others joined in the chorus of ideas.

'The worst problem of all,' he continued, 'is the fact that inevitably wine labels will become detached. Until the bottles are opened, positive identification will be impossible.'

Gloom settled over the assembly as the full magnitude of the disaster became apparent.

'They're going to be saddled with a heck of a lot of blind tastings,' remarked a man in the front row.

'Exactement!'

'Looking on the bright side,' Colonel Massingham rose to his feet, 'does it not also suggest a simple answer to the problem we are meant to be discussing. That of gridlock. Gridlock in cities only arises because a large number of people all want to go in different directions at the same time. Gridlock in the cellar arises out of a desire by many people for neatness – putting a case of twelve bottles of wine into a single row – either vertically or horizontally. Surely, in these days of computerisation that is an unnecessary constriction . . .'

While Colonel Massingham was talking, Monsieur Pamplemousse allowed his attention to wander. There would be no stopping the Colonel once he got the bit between his teeth.

Martin hurried through the saloon on his way forward. Misreading the situation, he raised his eyebrows sympathetically. Monsieur Pamplemousse held his hands apart, palm uppermost, with an air of resignation, although in fact he was only too happy to opt out of his responsibilities.

'. . . an elegant solution might be to devise a system – much as they do in theatres – where letters of the alphabet going in one direction are combined with seat numbers running at right angles. Provided the entries on the computer are kept up to date, individual bottles can be placed anywhere you like in the system and committed to the computer's memory. It is only a matter of calling them up when necessary . . .'

Sensing a change in the sound of the engine, Monsieur Pamplemousse realised *Le Creuset* was about to enter another lock. He suddenly remembered Pommes Frites.

'. . . mind if I use your blackboard, old boy?'

'*Avec plaisir.*' Monsieur Pamplemousse bowed to Colonel Massingham, converting his negative response to Martin into a more expansive gesture of welcome.

Taking advantage of the diversion, he slipped out through the door of the saloon onto the deck and made his way towards the front of the vessel. He was just in time, for *Le Creuset* was already nosing its way gently towards the gates at the far end of the lock. As the inside of the saloon behind him grew dark someone switched on a spotlight over the blackboard.

Martin held up his hand to signal stop – from his position behind the galley it was impossible for Sven to see the prow. Taking advantage of the flurry of activity, Monsieur Pamplemousse leant over the side of the rail. He breathed a sigh of relief. The rounded granite corner at the entrance to the lock, worn smooth by countless encounters over the years with other, less well handled craft, was achieving what human hands had earlier failed to do. Slowly and inexorably, as *Le Creuset* pulled against the mooring rope already wound in a slip knot round a bollard, the stern swung back against the wall of the lock and acted as a giant ram. It was only a matter of moments before the inevitable happened and Pommes Frites disappeared into the bowels of the barge.

Monsieur Pamplemousse crossed himself, offering up a silent prayer of thanks on behalf of his friend. What with one thing and another Saint Francis, patron saint of *chiens,* must be having a busy morning.

He glanced back towards the saloon. Colonel Massingham was in his element, and for the time being at least all eyes were on the blackboard as he expounded at length on his theory.

Making his way down the stairs and along the companionway on the lower deck, Monsieur

Pamplemousse had almost reached his quarters when he noticed the door to the adjoining cabin was slightly ajar. He paused as a wild thought entered his mind. Had the occupant been upstairs? He couldn't remember. There was one sure way to find out.

He gave the door a gentle tap. It moved slightly, but otherwise there was no noticeable response.

Glancing quickly over his shoulder to make sure no one else was around, he gave a push. The door swung open freely to his touch. The cabin was in darkness. The curtains over both portholes were tightly drawn. He slipped inside, closing the door behind him with his foot. As he turned and felt for the light switch he experienced a sharp pain in his ear, almost as though the lobe had been gripped by a pair of pincers. Instinctively reaching up to brush away what he assumed was an insect, he nearly jumped out of his skin as his hand made contact with human flesh and he felt a tongue, moist and probing, enter his right auricle.

Arms encircled him, holding him tightly in their grasp. Momentarily caught off balance, he found himself being half carried, half dragged across the room. It crossed his mind to wonder fleetingly if he had returned to his own cabin by mistake; or whether he was caught up in some wild dream. But it was all too real; he could hear the sound of rushing water outside as the lock began to fill. Toppling forwards out of control, he overbalanced and in reaching out to save himself encountered a pearl necklace.

Hands reached out and clasped his, tearing them away and forcing them remorselessly downwards on a slow and undulating journey until, accompanied by a succession of moans and groans of ecstasy, they reached their destination. Having lingered there for a short but undeniably pleasurable while, they were led onwards yet again, between silk and flesh until the two parted company and the former went its separate way.

The same guiding hands, having released his, then began expertly searching for other targets nearer home. Closing his eyes, Monsieur Pamplemousse tried thinking of France and of President Chirac, whilst at the same time making a mental note of where the garments had landed. There was a price to pay for everything in this world, and if it were a case of supply and demand, then so be it. Statistically, he would have to accept the possibility of becoming yet another anonymous victim of market forces calling the tune.

'Ssh!' Monsieur Pamplemousse managed a strangled cry.

He was in no position to put a finger to his lips, but the cries of 'Take me! Take me!' were becoming too loud for comfort. Any moment now someone was going to start banging on the dividing wall; or worse still, from the floor above. He was doing his best.

And then, as suddenly as it had begun, it was all over. His assailant gave a final shudder and pushed him away.

As the figure beneath him rose from the bed it felt as though a sudden hailstorm had broken out. A spattering of tiny round objects landed on his head. Reaching up, he parted the curtains and saw the boat had already reached the top of the lock. Through the gap a rain-soaked concrete tortoise stared him in the eye.

He heard a gasp from behind.

'You!' The woman stared at him. 'I thought . . .' She shook her head and screwed her eyes tightly shut for a moment or two as she fought to regain her composure.

'Never mind,' she said at last.

Given the circumstances, it struck Monsieur Pamplemousse as an odd comment to make. It was the nearest thing he had ever come to being ravished and all she could think of to say was 'never mind'; a typical piece of British understatement uttered in the clipped tones of her class. As if that made everything all right.

He bent down and under the guise of looking for pearls found what he was looking for. 'May I? A little souvenir to remember this moment by.' In the circumstances he felt it was the least she could do.

Mrs Massingham gave a curt nod and held the door open for him, her free hand clutching her naked throat.

A moment later he was outside in the corridor. It was as though the whole thing had never happened.

Staggering on his way, Monsieur Pamplemousse recalled Truffert's theory that some women went to pieces the moment they got on board ship. According to him, older married ones were often the worst. Truffert should know; he had spent some time in the Merchant Navy, had signed on for three more years when in fact his tour was up. But a canal boat?

Reaching the comparative safety of his own cabin, he was about to enter it when he heard another door being opened at the far end of the companionway. Looking round, he saw Boniface emerge from his quarters. He must have come on board again at the last stop. He had a furtive, tiptoeing air about him, as though about to embark on a pre-arranged rendezvous. Seeing Monsieur Pamplemousse, he gave a start, waved nervously, then disappeared back the way he had come.

Monsieur Pamplemousse put two and two together and made five, deducting two for bad timing.

Abeille was lying on his bed reading a book with a lurid cover. Pommes Frites lay stretched out beside her, licking himself. They both looked up as he entered. If Pommes Frites had suffered at all from his unhappy experience there were no visible signs; rather to the contrary – he looked extremely happy with his lot, as well he might. Certainly his tail was still in good working order.

'You were quick,' said Abeille. 'Don't say you've given the talk already?'

'I have sub-contracted,' said Monsieur Pamplemousse. 'It is in good hands. In the meantime I have a little present for you. I am afraid it is somewhat minimal, but it was the best I could do in the circumstances.'

'Gee!' Abeille sat up and ran her fingers expertly through the soft silk. 'Janet Reger.

'Hey!' Her expression suddenly changed. 'They're still warm!'

Leaping to her feet, she made for the open porthole and threw the garments out. 'What do you take me for?' she demanded shrilly. 'Some kind of hooker? Where did you get them, huh?'

'Ssh!' Monsieur Pamplemousse looked round nervously.

'Was that you banging away next door?' demanded Abeille.

'It was for your sake,' said Monsieur Pamplemousse simply. 'Please do not think for one moment that I was enjoying myself.'

'For *my* sake? Hogwash!' Abeille flung herself back down on the bed and grabbed her book.

Monsieur Pamplemousse resisted the temptation to point out that she was holding it upside down. 'Are you cross about something?' he asked.

'Me? Cross? No, why should I be?' She turned a page.

Monsieur Pamplemousse gazed at her indignantly.

Given all he had just been through, it would have been nice to receive a modicum of thanks for his pains rather than brickbats.

"'Blow, blow thou winter wind, thou art not so unkind as man's ingratitude".'

It was one of only two English quotations he could remember from his school days and the first time he'd ever had an opportunity to make use of it.

'Come again?' At least it had caught her attention.

'Shakespeare,' said Monsieur Pamplemousse.

'Yeah? I might have known. That's the kind of thing he would say. I bet he didn't have to wait around in his birthday suit for hours on end before he thought it up either.'

She was about to turn over another page when they both heard a familiar voice in the corridor outside.

'Hunn! Is that you, Hunn?'

'Jesus!' hissed Abeille. 'Not again.'

Leaping from the bed she made a wild dash for the safety of the shower. As the light came on and water flowed, Monsieur Pamplemousse began removing his trousers. It was a purely reflex action, the only thing to do in the circumstances, but he was beginning to feel more and more as though he had been caught up in a Feydeau farce from which there was no escape.

Alive to the general panic, Pommes Frites sprang into action on his own account and made a dive for the nearest porthole. His judgement and sense of timing were as impeccable as ever, but back legs scrabbling for a foothold on the bedhead testified to the fact that the net result was clearly a mirror image of his earlier effort.

The door opened and JayCee entered. He stared at Monsieur Pamplemousse.

'What are you?' he demanded. 'Some kind of water freak? You're worse than Boniface . . .'

'Cleanliness,' said Monsieur Pamplemousse virtuously, 'is next to godliness.'

'Yeah? Remind me to get you a peg for the halo.' JayCee looked around suspiciously. 'I thought I heard voices . . .'

Voices?' Monsieur Pamplemousse pretended he was having trouble with his shirt buttons, but he needn't have bothered. JayCee's mind was already elsewhere.

'How come you get your décor changed regularly?' he demanded.

Monsieur Pamplemousse glanced up, fearing the worst, but as ever Pommes Frites was proving more than equal to the situation.

Although not blessed with hindsight in the strictly literal sense, he must have brought an element of canine extra-sensory perception into play, for his summing up of the situation was faultless; his pose would undoubtedly have been an award-winning entry in any taxidermists' convention.

JayCee took a closer look. 'Reversible trophies! What'll they dream up next?

'You know something? I've only got one complaint. They shoulda stuffed it with the tail down instead of stuck up in the air, right? It's like having a guy with only one eye follow you around the room wherever you go . . .'

Fearing that JayCee might take it into his head to probe still further, Monsieur Pamplemousse hastily placed himself in front of Pommes Frites.

'Cyclops?' he ventured.

'No. Like I said, it was a guy with only one eye. Lon Chaney junior, that's it. It was in a film.'

Monsieur Pamplemousse gave up.

'No luck with Hunn?' asked JayCee.

'The last time I saw her she was reading a book,' said Monsieur Pamplemousse.

'She was?' JayCee could hardly have looked more surprised if he had heard an announcement heralding the Second Coming. 'All by herself?'

'Alone and unaided,' said Monsieur Pamplemousse truthfully. '*Pardonnez-moi . . .*' Taking the bull by the horns, he removed the last of his clothing.

'Yeah!' JayCee took the point. 'Don't let me stop you.' He looked at his watch. 'I guess maybe you got a point. There's nothing else to do. If you see Hunn, tell her I'm taking a shower.'

The door had hardly closed when a hand appeared round the side of the shower curtain, 'Come on in,' hissed Abeille. 'The water's fine.' She sounded her old self again.

But Monsieur Pamplemousse was already starting to get dressed. He had other things on his mind.

Abeille gave a pout. 'Don't tell me you've got a headache.'

'Worse,' said Monsieur Pamplemousse. Having made an abortive attempt at pulling Pommes Frites free, he realised he was starting to ache all over, but there was no point in elaborating.

Opening up *Le Guide*'s emergency case he worked swiftly, removing the items he needed, arranging them in a neat row along the dressing table; one tiny folding plastic cape – a miracle of twentieth-century petro-chemical compactness; a small transparent pack containing a dark substance – there was an 'eat by' date stamped on the bottom, but time had eroded it; a multi-purpose knife, and a tiny folding saw. He doubted if Monsieur Hippolyte Duval would have approved of the use to which he was about to put the last three items, but it was a case of needs must.

'You know one of the most depressing things in this world?' Abeille appeared behind him. 'Wanting to dry yourself and finding all you've got is a wet towel from the last time you took a shower.'

Having answered her own question, she stared across at Pommes Frites. 'JayCee's right. That's creepy. Can't you do something?'

Recognising his master's touch, Pommes Frites obligingly lowered his tail.

'I tell you the second most depressing thing,' said

142

Abeille, as she arranged some pillows to support Pommes Frites' feet. 'That's talking to yourself.'

She peered over Monsieur Pamplemousse's shoulder as he began sawing at the black material. 'Are you taking up model-making or something?'

'I am making a wedge for the door,' said Monsieur Pamplemousse, 'so that you will be safe while I am away.'

'You're leaving me?' said Abeille plaintively. 'Like this?'

'I have to if you want clothes,' said Monsieur Pamplemousse. 'Besides, there are things to do. I will be as quick as I can.'

'Great! Big deal!' Abeille glanced towards the open case. 'Do you have any other goodies in there? Like a bar of candy?'

Monsieur Pamplemousse shook his head. 'That will only make matters worse. It is the last thing he needs.'

'I wasn't thinking of Pommes Frites,' said Abeille. 'I was thinking of me. I haven't had any breakfast yet. I'd sell my soul for a peanut butter and jelly sandwich.'

'You are welcome to these.' Monsieur Pamplemousse pointed to a small pile of dried prune shavings, the result of several minutes' concentrated sawing.

'I cannot recommend them. It is what is known as "Compressed Emergency Rations".'

'Compressed' was a masterpiece of understatement.

It had been one of the original items in the kit, a throwback from the days when transport was in its infancy and inspectors sometimes found themselves stranded for days on end. One particularly bad winter Didier had been marooned in the Alps and had broken two teeth on his. He hadn't been able to face a prune since.

Abeille peered out through the remaining porthole. 'Looks like we're getting near another lock.'

'Good.' While she was otherwise engaged. Monsieur Pamplemousse emptied the contents of his washbag over the dressing table and began replacing them with the things he needed. Opening his case again, he took out a large Jiffy bag, measured it against the parrot for size, then wrote an address on the front.

'See you . . .' Abeille blew him a kiss as he made to leave.

Monsieur Pamplemousse placed the completed wedge on the floor by the door. 'Don't forget to use it.'

'If things get desperate,' said Abeille, 'I may even eat it.'

Taking advantage of the fact that *Le Creuset* was still working her way up the valley, which meant he would be temporarily out of sight of the other passengers when they entered the lock, Monsieur Pamplemousse unfolded the cape and slipped it over his head; it was better than nothing. He selected a bicycle from a pile on the sun deck, wiped the saddle dry, then carried it over his shoulder up an iron-runged ladder to the unrailed roof area above the saloon and waited while the boat came to a complete stop before stepping off.

Martin was already in deep conversation with the lock-keeper. When he saw Monsieur Pamplemousse he waved him over.

'There is a message for you. Will you please telephone your office. It's marked URGENT.'

Monsieur Pamplemousse hesitated. It was the last thing he wanted to hear. On the other hand . . . The lock-keeper was already leading the way into his cottage. Neither he nor his wife looked best pleased at the interruption to their routine.

'You will make sure you reverse the charges.' It was a command rather than a request.

'*Oui.*' Monsieur Pamplemousse called the operator and asked for a PCV call to Paris. While he waited he added some coins to a glass jar standing alongside the phone. The atmosphere eased a little.

The Director must have been sitting with his hand at the ready, for he answered almost immediately.

'Pamplemousse! How are you? Getting plenty of sunshine and rest, I trust.'

'It is pouring with rain, *Monsieur*, and I am about to set off on a *bicyclette* with a dead parrot.'

'Good. Good.' Clearly the Director was concentrating more on his own problems than other people's. Enquiries were a mere formality.

145

'And how is Pommes Frites?'

'He is stuck in a porthole.'

There was a slight pause as his words sunk in. 'This is not very heartening news, Pamplemousse. Do I take it that your voyage is not an unqualified success?'

'It has had its problems, *Monsieur*, but I am dealing with them as fast as they arise.'

'Excellent! Excellent! In that case, I am sure you won't mind if I burden you with one more. It concerns Chantal's aunt, Madame Ambert.'

Monsieur Pamplemousse held back the response he'd been about to make and awaited developments.

'I understand you have yet to make contact . . .'

'I was not aware, *Monsieur*, of any obligation on my part to do so. You simply suggested it would be a good idea should the opportunity arise. So far that hasn't happened.'

'Chantal is very upset, Aristide. She was hoping you might effect an introduction yesterday evening.'

Monsieur Pamplemousse fell silent. Suddenly it all began to fit into place; the look Madame Leclercq had given him after his accident in the Boulevard Haussman; the way she had momentarily held his hand; the haste with which the trip had been organised, as though every moment counted; the Director's insistence on secrecy. It followed a not unfamiliar pattern.

'Do I take it, *Monsieur*, that there are reasons

other than re-designing *Le Guide*'s logo for our being here? Pommes Frites will not be pleased if he feels he is being taken advantage of unnecessarily.'

The Director gave an audible sigh. 'It was not my idea, Pamplemousse, I assure you. I fought against it, but Chantal wouldn't listen. Unfortunately fate stepped in. I had already been discussing my thoughts with her. Our chance encounter in the Boulevard Haussman set the seal. The die was cast. It all goes back to that time when you came to her rescue in St George-sur-Lie. She has held you in high esteem ever since.'

'You mean that strange affair of the aunt who stumbled across all those aphrodisiacs, *Monsieur*? I remember it well. Have you heard from her lately?'

Realising the lock-keeper's wife was displaying more than a passing interest in his end of the conversation, Monsieur Pamplemousse turned away. *Le Creuset* had already moved out of the lock and was taking on water at a separate mooring just outside.

Doubtless the Director was telling the truth when he said the prime object of the exercise was as he had described it in his office, but . . .

'What is it you wish me to do, *Monsieur*?'

'Chantal would look upon it as a great favour if you could find time to visit her aunt. She is in need of help . . . things have deteriorated since we last spoke . . . there has been an incident . . .'

'An incident, *Monsieur*? You mean last night, at the pageant?'

'This morning . . . an incident at the winery.'

'You use the word "incident", *Monsieur*. Do you mean an accident?'

'No, Pamplemousse, I mean an incident. An accident is an unpremeditated happening. The word incident implies malice aforethought. The police have been informed, but there are things they do not, *must* not know. Things that are none of their business. That is where I hope you will come in, with your vast experience in these matters . . .'

'What matters, *Monsieur*?'

'Someone has been found in a wine press . . .'

'Squashed?' It seemed an obvious, yet not unreasonable question.

'Not irreparably. Fortunately some object or other got in the way before that could happen, but the poor fellow has been taken to hospital in a severe state of shock. He is under heavy sedation.'

Monsieur Pamplemousse resisted the temptation to suggest that it might have added body to the wine. Clearly the chief was in no mood for cheap jokes.

'Where is Madame Leclercq's aunt now, *Monsieur*?'

'She is at the winery.'

'Tell her I will telephone as soon as possible. There are a few things I must attend to first, but . . .'

'Thank you, Aristide. You are a good fellow.' For once the Director sounded truly grateful. Monsieur Pamplemousse couldn't help reflecting that he probably had good reason to be. Madame Leclercq was blessed with an abundance of charm, but he wouldn't like to stand in her way if she had her mind set on something.

As he rode off into the rain Monsieur Pamplemousse glanced back over his shoulder towards *Le Creuset*. Colonel Massingham was still giving his lecture. Pommes Frites was watching his master's departure through the porthole. He didn't look too unhappy. Doubtless a passing rabbit would provide him with the necessary impetus to wriggle free if and when he felt like it. For the time being at least his rear end was in the dry; which was more than Monsieur Pamplemousse could say for his own. A trickle of rain was already running down behind the collar of his cape.

Abeille waved from the adjoining porthole. He returned it.

The curtains in the next cabin remained tightly drawn. He wondered if Mrs Massingham had managed to find all her pearls. A little way along the towpath he passed the spot where her *culottes* had landed; a tiny patch of white amongst the reeds and too far away to be rescued even if he had felt inclined to try.

Head down, his eyes firmly fixed on the waterlogged towpath ahead, Monsieur Pamplemousse pedalled on his way. He had other, more important things in mind.

CHAPTER SIX

Some twenty minutes later Monsieur Pamplemousse reappeared along the towpath, heading back the way he had come. As he had feared, *Le Creuset* was nowhere to be seen.

There was no sign of the lock-keeper either, or his wife. Their cottage door was shut, which wasn't altogether surprising. Apart from the one launch, he had seen no other sign of movement on the canal that morning.

Having no great desire to ask if he might use their phone again, Monsieur Pamplemousse pedalled on his way, aiming to stop at the next place where he could make a call in reasonable privacy.

Drawing a blank on Abeille's clothes had been an unforeseen set-back. He was positive he had found the place where they had landed; the tree and its surroundings were etched on his memory like a bad dream. Either they had been blown off the branch by the wind, or someone had got there first. If only Pommes Frites hadn't got himself stuck in the porthole he might have helped search the surrounding fields. But Pommes Frites wasn't with him. Pommes Frites knew which side his bread was buttered.

Perseverance received its just reward at Gissey-sur-Ouche. Propping his *bicyclette* up against a bus stop which boasted a telephone kiosk, Monsieur Pamplemousse picked his way gingerly over a manhole cover which had been forced out of its mounting by the heavy rain and dialled the number he had been given.

The Director had beaten him to it. Madame Ambert was expecting his call and had made arrangements to take him out to lunch.

'It will be easier to talk. Besides, I feel I owe you a proper meal after last night's travesty.' A car would pick him up.

Monsieur Pamplemousse was too wet to argue, and a bus shelter was better than nothing for the time being. Having described where he was, he hung up and took stock of his surroundings.

Alongside a timetable, which occupied most of a glass-encased notice board, there was a printed warning issued by the *Direction des Services Vétérinaires*. Anti-rabies tablets had been laid down near known habitats of foxes in the area. DO NOT TOUCH and DO NOT GATHER was the message they were trying to get across. The same body was carrying out a *dératinisation* in the district. It struck Monsieur Pamplemousse that nature was probably doing the job for them. Any self-respecting rat would be miles away by now, swimming for its life.

Taking advantage of a momentary easing of the rain, he set out on a brief voyage of exploration. It lasted all of five minutes. The high spot was a doorknocker made from the bleached skull of some unidentifiable animal. Having got as much mileage as he could out of it, Monsieur Pamplemousse returned to the bus shelter.

A notice from the *Militaire Territorial* warned of manoeuvres being carried out using *Armes de Guerre*. Bugles would be used to sound the retreat. Poor devils. He didn't fancy their lot.

A *Festival des Arts* was being held next month.

Somewhat improbably, strains of 'Auld Lang Syne' came from a radio in a nearby house. It was almost as bad as seeing a Papa Noël in July.

Monsieur Pamplemousse gazed out at the bleak scene and wondered what he was doing there. He toyed with the idea of phoning the Director back and saying enough was enough, but he knew he wouldn't.

A black Mercedes 300E turned off the main road and drew up beside him. Fabrice Delamain climbed out. He was wearing a brown leather jacket over an open-neck checked shirt and belted corduroy trousers; a very different image to the one he'd last seen in Beaune.

Waving aside Monsieur Pamplemousse's protests he opened the boot of the car, loaded up the cycle, then held open the passenger door.

Monsieur Pamplemousse removed his cape and made himself comfortable. 'You must have driven like the wind.'

Monsieur Delamain climbed in beside him and executed an immaculate U-turn.

'I was in Dijon. The lights were green.' As they drove back up to the D108 he picked up a telephone and dialled a number.

'I am just leaving Gissey . . . would you like us to go straight to the restaurant?

'*D'accord*. We will be there in thirty minutes.'

Fabrice Delamain drove fast, but cleanly and with precision, using the five speed gearbox effortlessly, as though it were an extension of his right arm.

Monsieur Pamplemousse immediately felt relaxed and at home with him. He wondered if he should broach the subject of the troubles chez Ambert, but decided against it. They would come out soon enough. He settled instead on discussing the problems of wine-making generally. It was always good to hear an expert's point of view.

'You must be cursing this weather.'

Fabrice shrugged. '*C'est la vie*. You learn to live with it. Nature doesn't offer a choice. It is also a challenge.'

'What is the saying?' Monsieur Pamplemousse hoped he had got it right. 'August makes the grape. September makes the wine.'

'We have many sayings in Burgundy. "*C'est l'homme qui fait la différence*" is another; "It is man who makes the difference". That appeals to me more. It massages my ego.

'Wine making happens only once a year and at that time everything must be right; the weather, the temperature, the ripeness of the fruit, the precise time of picking, the correct development of the yeasts, the temperature of the must – whether to heat it or cool it; you are lucky if you get seven out of ten. There are a thousand and one decisions to be made and they all have to be right, otherwise a year's work is wasted. Since the official date for the start of picking generally coincides with the autumn equinox, which often heralds a change in the weather, speed is of the essence.'

Keeping watch out of the window to his left as they drove parallel to the Canal de Bourgogne, Monsieur Pamplemousse thought he saw *Le Creuset* at one point, but it came and went in a flash. It was so easy to get used to the slower pace of life – it made the adjustment back to normal that much harder.

'In this business there are many things to worry

about besides the weather,' said Fabrice. 'People think we just plant vines, pick the grapes and turn them into wine. Believe me, it is an all-the-year round occupation. January is the only quiet month; a time for taking stock. We have to decide how many barrels to order – usually about twenty per cent are replaced each year. We now have our own wood from the Fôret de Bertranges, and this has to be cut and then put aside and dried for two years before it goes to be made into barrels.

'In February there is pruning to be done – everywhere you see smoke from burning cuttings – and people look forward to the arrival of the travelling Still.

'March is the time for ploughing; there is grafting to be done and the first of the fertilisers go down. In April we carry out the planting of new vines. All through the spring and during the summer there is weeding, fertilising, and more pruning. June is the really critical time, when the flowering takes place. That is when we hope for calm weather. Time is measured by the seasons, and each season has its problems.'

'You have been in it all your life?'

'And my father before me, and his father before that.'

'Always at Clos d'Ambert?'

'Always at Clos d'Ambert.'

'You must have seen many changes.'

'Many.' Fabrice turned off the main road, crossed the canal by a narrow bridge, slackened speed slightly as he drove through a small, deserted village, then headed towards the hills. 'When I was small there were fruit trees amongst the vines and at harvest time there was always a vast team of pickers. Now the trees have all been uprooted to allow free passage for the harvesting machine. We still use a few pickers but one machine can do the work of twenty. I have seen horses exchanged for tractors. Tractors are fine, but they are much more tiring; horses went at their own pace, but they knew every inch of the land; they did most of the work for you.

'In the old days we used to pick the grapes when the leaves started to change colour; now the vines are better cared for and the date is decided by analysis of the sugar and acid content of the grapes. When I first began, they were still trodden by humans – a century ago it was known as the *vigneron*'s annual bath time. Now we use a Bucher pneumatic press which has a throughput that is hard to keep pace with. We ferment the juice in computerised stainless steel vats . . .'

He broke off as they drove past a collection of stone houses, almost too small to be called a village, turned in through some imposing wrought iron gates, then followed a winding gravelled path leading to a larger building standing astride a narrow stream. A goat with yellowing teeth supervised their arrival over a neighbouring hedge as they drew up alongside another, older Mercedes. Monsieur Pamplemousse looked at his watch. It said 14.00. The journey had taken thirty minutes exactly.

His spirits rose as he saw the sign over the entrance. Taste buds began to make themselves felt. He remembered the hotel from an entry in *Le Guide*. The restaurant had two Stock Pots. Guillot still talked of the time when he had stayed there overnight and had caught a trout from his bedroom window. He had eaten it for lunch and he spoke in hushed tones of the memory. It was he who had recommended it for a second Stock Pot.

'You are not coming in?'

Fabrice shook his head. 'I have work to do.'

Monsieur Pamplemousse hesitated. 'Could you possibly do me a favour?' He handed Fabrice the package containing the parrot. 'Could you arrange for this to be sent by Chronopost? I want it to get there as soon as possible.'

Fabrice glanced at the address on the label. 'I will do even better. I am on my way to Beaune. I will take it for you.'

Monsieur Pamplemousse hesitated. 'In that case I suggest you simply leave it. There is no need to say who gave it to you.

'*À bientôt.*' They exchanged goodbyes.

As he walked towards the hotel, Monsieur Pamplemousse saw the reflection of the Mercedes' brake lights in the plate glass doors. They flicked on and off briefly as Fabrice Delamain negotiated the entrance gates. The plate glass doors parted as he drew near.

Madame Ambert was already seated when he entered the restaurant. She was talking to a man in white overalls Monsieur Pamplemousse assumed to be *le patron*.

He glanced round the room as the *maître d'hôtel* greeted him and led him towards the table. There were three other couples eating, all seated some distance apart. They looked as though they were nearing the end of their meal. All the same, it was good that it wasn't the kind of restaurant where everyone was grouped together for the sake of the management's convenience, come what may.

'I hope I haven't kept you.'

'On the contrary,' Madame Ambert held out her hand. 'I am surprised you got here so quickly.'

'Monsieur Delamain is a man of his word, but the weather didn't help.'

The chef made a face. 'The weather is affecting everything, *Monsieur. Bon appétit.*' Nodding to Monsieur Pamplemousse, he left the room.

A waiter appeared with a silver tray of *amuse gueules*; some tiny sausages in pastry and some *gougères* – cheese-flavoured sticks of *choux* pastry – golden-brown and crisp.

'I hope you will forgive me,' said Madame Ambert,

'but since it is late I have asked André to surprise us. I think you will not be disappointed.'

Monsieur Pamplemousse reached for the notebook he kept hidden inside a pocket in his right trouser leg. 'In that case I hope you will forgive *me* if I make notes.' It was an opportunity too good to miss.

Two glasses of champagne arrived at the table.

'With the compliments of Monsieur Delamain.' The *sommelier* bowed and withdrew.

Monsieur Delamain had clearly been busy with his mobile telephone again.

'You did not wish him to join us for lunch?' Monsieur Pamplemousse felt perhaps he should have insisted.

Madame Ambert shook her head. 'I doubt if he would have wanted to. Fabrice has been a naughty boy; he and a few others. It is a very close-knit community, but I have no doubt who was the ringleader. I should be very cross with him.'

'But you are not?'

'I have known Fabrice all my life. We were practically brought up together. I don't know what I would do without him. He is more than a *régisseur* – a manager – he is my guardian angel.'

It was a simple statement of fact. Monsieur Pamplemousse decided not to probe any further. The fact that Madame Ambert had suggested meeting on neutral territory suggested a certain reserve; a desire to get to know the person she was dealing with before lowering her guard.

One of the kitchen staff was fishing about with a net in an outside tank permanently fed by the stream – another addition since Guillot's day; gaining a second Stock Pot was an expensive business. Beyond the tank there was a vegetable garden. Unusually, considering the height above sea level, part of it was given over to the growing of vines.

Under cover of watching the man land one of the fish, Monsieur Pamplemousse took stock of his companion. At a guess Madame Ambert was in her mid-sixties. Well groomed, expensively dressed, although not outrageously so. The few jewels she wore – a gold watch, a diamond ring on her left hand, necklace, brooch – were all of modern design. Quiet good taste was the best way to put it.

Monsieur Pamplemousse took an immediate liking to her. Perhaps it was the laugh lines each side of her brown eyes that did the trick; her face lit up when she smiled. Although her hair was immaculately coiffed there was no attempt at concealing its greyness. One thing was certain, the Director's aunt was not the sort of person who would take kindly to being questioned. On the surface at least, she was very self-assured. He would need to tread carefully.

They sat in silence for a moment or two while the *sommelier* presented a bottle of wine in a silver cooler; an '89 Bâtard Montrachet from Olivier Leflaive.

Madame Ambert found a hint of nectarine in the finish, Monsieur Pamplemousse elicited honey and lime. Both agreed it more than lived up to its maker's reputation. He wondered what verdict Abeille's electronic analyser would deliver, or what Madame Ambert might have to say about such an unholy device.

A team of waiters arrived bearing the result of the fishing activities.

'C'est très chaud, Monsieur.' The waiter anticipated Monsieur Pamplemousse's intention as he laid the plate before him. Points were added below the starched white tablecloth.

Fried in a light coating of oil and flour, the outside of the trout was crisp and golden, the parsley butter hot and foaming as it should be. It came with a simple dish of *pommes purée* and a sauceboat of melted butter. Although beautifully clean, the potatoes tasted as though they had been boiled in their skins to preserve the flavour. It was the mark of a perfectionist chef who took endless trouble. Lemon juice had been added to the butter.

As they finished the wine Madame Ambert held forth on the importance of knowing who were the best producers.

'Burgundy is different to any other region of France. Bordeaux is made up of large vineyards, many of which are owned either by corporations or banks. They are heavily financed, prestige operations well able to withstand the ups and downs of the market. The people who make the TGV, for example, also own Château Gruaud-Larose. Money is no object. They are the glamorous side of the business.

'For historical reasons Burgundy is made up of many tiny parcels of land. Over the years the land has become fragmented by inheritance and most of the growers are small. Clos de Vougeot is a good example; 123 acres with 85 owners. Like many peasant farmers, they do everything. In the day they work in the fields; in the evening they work in the cellars; at night they do the books. At the end of it all some of them make a little wine for themselves and their friends, but most sell the grapes or the juice on to people like ourselves or Leflaive. Apart from our vineyard in Chambertin we have a few parcels of land in other *appellations,* but mostly we buy in. Pinot noir is a very fickle grape. Knowing which growers are good and which are not, those who can be trusted and those who can't, is knowledge beyond price and it works both ways. Trust is a very special commodity. That is one of the things Fabrice brings to the company.'

She broke off as an '88 Chambertin Clos d'Ambert-Celeste was brought to replace the now empty bottle of Bâtard Montrachet. Having shown it to Madame Ambert with all the reverence of his calling, the *sommelier* withdrew to a small table in the middle of the dining-room. Decanted, tasted and approved, glasses filled, the bottle and the cork were left on the table alongside the decanter.

Escargots à la façon d'un gourmand arrived; snails as the connoisseur likes them. They had been cooked in the classic gourmet manner that had earned the dish its name; in meat jelly and butter, with truffles, chopped parsley, garlic, and a sprinkling of breadcrumbs added at the last moment.

They were the best he had tasted for many a year; beautifully fat and piping hot; still sizzling in their dish.

'André rears them on his own organically grown vines. He finds the pinot noir grape gives them their special flavour.'

Monsieur Pamplemousse made a note in his book. It was what France was all about; France and *Le Guide.*

The *pintade rôti* which followed was exquisitely, deceptively simple. A guinea-fowl stuffed with liver, rosemary and thyme, roasted and served with potatoes which had been cooked in the same baking tray. Each plate was decorated with a single lettuce leaf, crisply fresh from the garden. Pommes Frites would have signalled his approval. But then Pommes Frites would have approved of the whole thing, probably rounding things off afterwards with a romp in the stream, trying to catch his own trout.

Monsieur Pamplemousse congratulated Madame Ambert on the wine. 'It is very elegant,' he said. 'You must feel rewarded.'

Madame Ambert acknowledged the compliment. 'It is just ready for drinking but it has many years of life yet. It has good "weight" in the mouth. All the flavours are present: raspberry, cherry . . . plum. They almost mask the tannin, but it is there. In a few years' time it should be even better.'

She lowered her glass and viewed it against the white tablecloth. 'It is a little hazy, but that is because we do not filter. Fabrice refuses to – he says it removes some of the natural qualities of the wine.'

Monsieur Pamplemousse listened with interest, but all the same he couldn't help wondering when they would get down to business.

It was reminiscent of the time, some years earlier, when he had taken early retirement from the *Sûreté* and the Director had offered him a job with *Le Guide*. He had found himself working his way through a vast lunch wondering why he was there and which course would produce the moment of truth. In the Director's case it had been over the second cup of coffee.

He picked up the empty bottle and studied the label. Madame Ambert's name appeared in isolation at the bottom. It seemed as good a time as any to bring the matter up.

'May I ask if that was your brother sitting beside you at yesterday evening's pageant?'

'Dominique?' She nodded.

'How long has he been part of your company?'

Madame Ambert hesitated before gently correcting him. '*Our* company.' It was as though she had swallowed something that left a nasty taste. 'Under French law, when Papa died the estate was divided between the two of us. Strictly speaking his name ought always to have been on the label, but since to all intents and purposes he had disappeared off the face of the earth, it never happened.'

'When did your father die?'

'Soon after the war.'

'And your mother?'

'She died during the war. I think they both, in their different ways and for different reasons, died of a broken heart.

'Dominique went to school in Dijon. He was arrested in 1941 along with four other classmates for persistent singing of the British national anthem.

'He was taken to the rue Docteur-Chassier . . .'

'The Gestapo headquarters?'

'Number 9 *bis*. There used to be a plaque marking the spot, but it has gone now.

'He had already been caught red-handed once before, standing in front of a blackboard with the chalk in his hand. Some other boy – Dominique denied all responsibility – had drawn the Cross of Lorraine on the board. The "V-campaign" was at its height and he was eventually deported along with the rest to "finish his studies" in Germany. I remember crying myself to sleep.'

Monsieur Pamplemousse nodded. It brought back memories of his own wartime childhood. The list of 'crimes' was endless: everything from spitting at German soldiers, jostling the officers, not replying quickly enough to questions, hoisting the French flag without permission, listening to foreign radio stations, smuggling letters, delivering tracts, reading books like *All Quiet on the Western Front*. Punishment ranged from a 'going over' by the Gestapo to the death penalty.

He reached for the decanter in order to replenish their glasses and was beaten to it by the *sommelier*, who appeared as if from nowhere. The better the restaurant the harder it was to have a private conversation. At least the wine hadn't been taken off to a separate table out of anyone's reach except the staff.

'And when the war ended?'

'He survived. You could say he was the lucky one – the others died in a concentration camp – but when he returned he was not the same person who had left us. He had grown up and he had learnt all the tricks. He found it hard to settle down. I think perhaps he had suffered a lot and he was determined to make up for it. He stuck it at home for six months and then he made tracks for America. Papa was heartbroken; he had always pictured Dominique taking over the vineyard. He had plans for him to go to the *Lycée Viticole* in Beaune, and afterwards on a tour of the world to see how people did things elsewhere. Instead of which,' she shrugged, 'it was left to me.

'It was not easy for a woman in those days. It had always been predominantly a man's world and you had to be tough to succeed. It went against my nature. Now, there are many others, from Lalou Bize-Leroy here in Burgundy to Madame Mentzelopoulos and her daughter at Château Margaux in Bordeaux . . .'

'But now your brother has come back to claim his share of the property?'

'Dominique has totally different ideas about what should be done. He is very commercial. He speaks a foreign language in more ways than one. He is full of phrases like "capital formation" and "maximising our potential". You will have seen what is happening at our offices in Beaune, but it is worse at the vineyard.

'We have moved with the times, but we still try to produce wine the old way. That is the French way of doing things. As a nation we love progress. We are always eager to embrace the latest invention, but at the same time we do not throw out the old without good reason.

'Dominique has only been here five minutes and already he is talking of having his own image on the bottle! He wants to throw the *château* open, take in guests, open up a shop – make more commercial wine which matures earlier. He wants it filtered so that he can take advantage of the American market. If a wine does not arrive in America crystal clear there are problems with the health regulations. We have always used vats that have been properly aged so that the taste of the oak does not predominate and denature the wine. He wishes to change that too.'

'In short,' he said, 'your brother wants to follow the market trends rather than lead them. Sadly, that is the same in many areas.'

Madame Ambert nodded. 'I am afraid he is resented. In this part of the world you have to earn people's respect, otherwise they can make the going very hard. There are those winemakers in Bourgogne who, for want of a better description, are in the tourist trade. They would argue that they are helping to spread the light, and no doubt there is a certain amount of truth in that; there is good and bad in everything.

'But either way you should be true to yourself and to your customers. To me, making good wine is the beginning and end of everything. What Dominique is doing is selling off the family silver and that won't last for ever.'

Monsieur Pamplemousse thought of the pruning shears manufactured in China and mentally substituted 'hasn't lasted' for 'won't last'.

He watched Madame Ambert while she was talking. In some respects it all added up: the return of the ne'er do well, the upheaval it had caused, the arguments and the recriminations. But . . . But, someone had made an attempt to kill someone else . . .

The cheese trolley arrived and broke up the conversation. Madame Ambert chose a local Epoisse, waving aside the others. Monsieur Pamplemousse followed suit. It was one of the few good cheeses made in a region given over to vines rather than grazing. Cured in humid cellars for three months, with frequent washings in Burgundy, it was smooth without being cloying. Overall, there was a spicy, tangy flavour which complemented the last of the wine. Doubtless that was the main reason why, over the years, it had evolved the way that it had; to complement wine.

Fabrice Delamain had painted a vivid picture of immutable laws, of changes brought about slowly with the passage of time. Old habits died hard and people were naturally resistant to change, but the kind of things Madame Ambert had been talking about were hardly likely to make people start taking pot shots at each other. Or were they? There was a lot of money tied up in the cellars in Beaune. Probably a lot of undercurrents too.

One way and another Burgundy had acquired a bad reputation in the period after the war. The very nature of the way it was organised, the complexities of land ownership, where one vineyard could have a dozen different owners, laid it open to abuse. Who knew what went on after dark in some of the cellars? Who could say for certain, hand on heart, that the label on the barrel was always a wholly honest description of what it contained? Things were much better now, new laws had been brought in, but they weren't always easy to administer. In the end, as Madame Ambert rightly said, trust was of the utmost importance. It could take years to build up and then be lost overnight.

'Am I right in thinking you do not like your brother?'

She was immediately on her guard.

'Why should it be assumed that two people who have been apart for so many years should automatically like each other? Dominique is at best a faded memory. If I search my mind I can picture playing with him when I was small; but he was always telling tales and I was the one who got the blame. He is older than me and he used to go off and do other things.'

'But do you dislike him?' persisted Monsieur Pamplemousse.

'It is worse than that. I find I have no feelings for him one way or the other. Or rather I *had* no feelings until he turned up out of the blue. For years I heard nothing at all. Not even so much as a postcard to say he was alive and well. Now, he wishes to take over everything. If I am totally honest I would say I resent him because he represents a threat to all I believe in and have worked for. Apart from

171

which, I cannot stand the almost daily rows and recriminations.'

The meal ended as simply as it had begun; the mark of a confident chef who had no need to prove himself. White peaches poached in sweet champagne to which a vanilla pod had been added. Chilled and halved, the hollow of each had been filled with a mixture of grated and sugared strawberries, cream and lemon juice. The juice in which the peaches had been poached was served in a separate bowl.

'I trust you enjoyed it.'

Monsieur Pamplemousse made a final note, then closed his pad with a sigh. 'I will tell you what I have written. "It is a good restaurant. There is no deception. It did not disappoint".'

1 did not tell André who you are.'

'*Merci. Monsieur le Directeur* has a very high regard for anonymity. That, combined with total honesty in reporting and the preservation of established standards, are his three main preoccupations in life.'

Madame Ambert hesitated. 'Would you, in the interest of the last one in particular, whilst still maintaining the first two, be prepared to meet my brother?'

Monsieur Pamplemousse hesitated. He had a sudden mental picture of Abeille and Pommes Frites awaiting his return. 'Of course. It is, I suspect, the main reason why I am here. But today would be a problem.'

'Tomorrow is Sunday. That would be a good day. Everyone will be at the vineyard.'

'Tomorrow,' said Monsieur Pamplemousse.

'How shall I contact you?'

'I will telephone.' JayCee was right about one thing. Maintaining communications with the outside world was not what life on a canal barge was all about.

They both took *café* at the table and for a while the conversation turned to other topics. Eventually Madame Ambert excused herself and disappeared in the direction of the kitchen.

While she was gone Monsieur Pamplemousse toyed with the *petits fours*. Perhaps the Director's aunt was right. Sometimes to know more was to understand less. And yet . . . he couldn't rid himself of the feeling that she was holding back on him in some way; that he had yet to hear the whole story. Perhaps she wanted him to form his own opinion of her brother first.

When Madame Ambert returned she was wearing a coat and carrying a long plastic bag full of *escargots*, their marbled shells clearly visible as she held it up for him to see.

'A little gift from André and myself. I am so grateful you were able to come.'

Monsieur Pamplemousse was momentarily at a loss for words.

'Everything seems so closed in,' said Madame

Ambert. 'I cannot rid myself of the feeling that something dreadful is about to happen.

'Fabrice will take you where you wish to go. *À demain.* Until tomorrow.' She handed him a card with the telephone number of the vineyard. A moment later she was gone.

After what seemed an age he heard her car drive away and shortly afterwards Fabrice Delamain himself appeared. Presumably he and the Director's aunt must have spoken, for on the way back to his car he asked for Monsieur Pamplemousse's opinion of the wine.

It struck Monsieur Pamplemousse that the question had been posed out of politeness rather than any great desire to know. He seemed preoccupied, and as they set off even his driving felt mechanical, lacking its earlier *panache*.

Oui, he had delivered the parcel.

Non, he had spoken to no one.

There was no mention of his having looked inside the packet.

As with Madame Ambert, Monsieur Pamplemousse was left with the feeling of being an outsider. The earlier rapport they had established had gone.

'Where would you like me to take you?'

'There is no need to drive all the way back,' said Monsieur Pamplemousse. 'I have some shopping to do.'

If he had been totally honest he would have added

that he wouldn't have minded getting some fresh air. The rain seemed to have eased off for the moment and the atmosphere in the car was becoming more and more oppressive. It would be nice to have time to think; a little 'space'.

'Shopping?' Fabrice looked at him in surprise, as though he'd asked for a ticket to the moon.

'Ideally,' said Monsieur Pamplemousse, 'I need to visit a video store. That, and a shop where it would be possible to purchase a few items of clothing . . . ladies' clothing.'

Fabrice made a sucking noise. He seemed glad of the diversion; a problem to solve, however mundane it might be.

'A video shop . . . ladies clothing . . .'

'A present for my wife,' said Monsieur Pamplemousse by way of explanation.

'In Beaune or Dijon it would be no problem, but in the villages around here there are few shops. Mostly they have less than a hundred inhabitants. Even the *boulangers* deliver bread by van these days. Unless . . .'

Coming to an abrupt stop, he glanced up at his mirror. Now that he had something positive to think about his mood changed. Backing down the hill at high speed, he slid to a halt, then turned off to the right and they began climbing again through a forest of oak trees. The clouds were low overhead; all enveloping, adding to the feeling of claustrophobia.

'A few kilometres away, there is a possibility . . .'

'That is very kind of you.'

'I can wait for you . . .'

Monsieur Pamplemousse declined the offer. 'I have my *bicyclette*. It will do me good. After all that food . . .'

'You will find it is downhill for most of the way.'

'That sounds admirable,' said Monsieur Pamplemousse. It also sounded as though Fabrice was glad to be relieved of his task of acting as chauffeur. There was no question of arguing the matter.

They came out of the forest and almost immediately houses appeared on either side, their shutters closed against the weather. Fabrice parked the car in a deserted *place*.

'There!' He pointed towards a small shop. A neon sign above the door said *VIDEOS EXTRAORDINAIRES*.

Climbing out of the car, he went round to the back. Gathering up his belongings, the cape and the bag of *escargots,* Monsieur Pamplemousse followed suit.

By the time he caught up, his bicycle had already been removed.

'At least the rain has nearly stopped.'

'Nearly' was taking an optimistic view. Monsieur Pamplemousse donned his cape. Clearly, from the speed with which Fabrice closed the boot lid he was anxious to be on his way.

Glancing round the *place* Monsieur Pamplemousse

spotted the only other shop, directly opposite the first. It was called *PARIS MODES* and its frontage was almost identical, but the windows were dressed overall with fashions he hadn't seen in many a year. Chic was not a word which sprang to mind, and he regarded the display with a sinking heart.

Monsieur Delamain held out his hand. '*Bonne chance*,' he said wryly. 'I hope you get what you want.'

'*Merci*,' said Monsieur Pamplemousse dryly. '*Bonne journée*.'

He stood watching as Fabrice climbed back into the car and started the engine. As it purred into life the window slid open and a hand clutching a small white envelope reached out.

'I think perhaps you should see this. Later . . . at your leisure.'

Before Monsieur Pamplemousse had time to reply, the window slid shut again. He stood watching as the car disappeared into the gloom, heading back the way they had come. Fabrice was already on the telephone.

Propping the bicycle again a stone bollard, Monsieur Pamplemousse squeezed the envelope, registering the contents without for a moment betraying his mounting excitement, then consigned it to an inside pocket. The rain had started bucketing down again. Fabrice was right; it was something to be considered at leisure.

As he made his way across the *place* a sudden

gust of wind funnelling through a narrow gap between two buildings caught him by surprise. His cape billowed out like a sail as it propelled him inexorably towards his destination. But Monsieur Pamplemousse scarcely registered the fact. His mind was already racing ahead.

CHAPTER SEVEN

The proprietor of *Videos Extraordinaires* crawled out from his back parlour like a great fat slug. He didn't look best pleased at having been disturbed. Pointedly taking his time, he rubbed the sleep from his eyes, slowly filling the space behind the tiny counter before deigning to examine the cassette.

'*Monsieur* does not have the camera with him?'

Monsieur Pamplemousse confessed he hadn't. The last time he had seen it had been in the shower with Abeille, at which point his mind had been on other things.

The admission met with a prolonged intake of breath between yellowing teeth. 'It is VHS-C. To play this size of tape in a normal VHS recorder will require a special cassette adapter.'

'And you do not have one?'

'I have one, *Monsieur*,' the man pointed to a shelf on the wall behind him, 'but it is new and boxed. Once the box has been opened it will no longer be new.'

Holding the bag of *escargots* with one hand, Monsieur Pamplemousse went through the motions of groping inside his cape with the other, but any hopes he might have nursed that the man wouldn't want to see the colour of his money fell on stony ground.

'And if I decide to purchase one, may I view the tape in your shop?'

'*Naturellement, Monsieur.*' Having first completed the washing of his hands in invisible soap, the man pressed a key on his cash till. A flap bearing the figure 400fr appeared behind a window. His finger hovered over the NO SALE key. It was the price of progress – take it or leave it.

While the tape was being loaded Monsieur Pamplemousse took the opportunity to explore other avenues.

'I am told it is unusual in this part of the world to find a village with shops.'

'The winters can be hard, *Monsieur*. People need things to occupy their time, otherwise it hangs heavy on their hands. Both Dijon and Beaune are impossible to reach when the snow is bad.'

'Would there be anywhere I could buy a present for a lady? A clothes shop, *par exemple*?'

The man waved vaguely towards the far side of the *place*. '*Monsieur* should try *Paris Modes*.'

Monsieur Pamplemousse had half expected as much. His spirits fell at the thought of Abeille's reaction.

They perked up again as a television receiver on the far side of the shop sprang to life. Viewed on a Philips 84 cm screen, the shots of the previous evening's pageant positively leapt out at him; colour gave the tape another dimension; 40 watts of hifi stereophonic sound, relayed through a battery of speakers and sub woofers, added yet a third. If there had been room in the shop to stand back without coming up against racks of video cassettes, batteries, plugs, cables and sundry other items, the overall effect could hardly have been improved had the tape been projected in a cinema on the Champs Elysées.

It began where he had left off earlier in the day, so he asked the man to rewind it slightly, stopping him at a point shortly before Vert-Vert's arrival in Nantes.

Seeing the candlelit corridors of the cellars, Monsieur Pamplemousse found himself comparing them with the catacombs in Paris, that depository of ancient remains, where femurs and tibias rather than bottles of Burgundy were neatly stacked along the walls. During the war the catacomb's labyrinth of tunnels had been put to good use by members of the

181

Resistance, who had used it as their headquarters. In much the same way, it would be possible for a person to come and go unobserved for hours on end in the cellars below the *negociants'* offices in Beaune; a fact which was convincingly demonstrated a few moments later as Abeille panned away from the group of nuns to see the ship arriving, then almost immediately panned back again.

As he watched Monsieur Pamplemousse realised something he hadn't noticed before. During the time it took to complete the movement – perhaps all of ten seconds – the twelve nuns became thirteen. Until that moment he had assumed there had been thirteen nuns right from the start. He could have kicked himself for not checking something so basic. It only went to show that one should never take anything for granted. It also meant that the person infiltrating the group must have done so for not much more than a minute or so at the most.

He watched the pageant unfold: the camera zooming out to include the parrot, the moment when Vert-Vert took off and fluttered into the air, faltered for a second, then plummeted down to the bottom of the frame as Abeille zoomed in for a close-up. He had seen the latter half before, of course, and was prepared, but on the larger screen when the camera panned back to the group, it was obvious there were now only twelve. He wondered if the thirteenth person had been watching Abeille and whoever it was had seized their chance to come and go while she was pointing the camera away from them, or whether it had been sheer luck rather than good timing.

'*Excusez-moi, Monsieur.*'

Monsieur Pamplemousse picked up the remote controller and ran the tape back until it reached the point where the extra nun appeared for the first time, then pressed the button marked still frame. Magnified in colour on the giant screen the picture revealed something else he hadn't spotted earlier. Protruding at around waist level from the habit of the new arrival, blued metal against dark grey, was the unmistakable business end of a gun.

Monsieur Pamplemousse stared at it for a long while. It put an entirely different complexion on things. Far from Vert-Vert having got in the way of a shot fired by someone in the audience, it looked as though the reverse must have happened.

He would have given anything to have been blessed with X-ray eyes so that he could see through the habit – or better still, ten seconds with an X-ray machine at an airport in order to make a positive identification of the weapon. It looked more like an air gun than the kind of revolver one might have expected; possibly, from the partridge style front sight, a single shot Crossman target pistol operated by compressed air. That would explain why no one had heard a shot being fired or seen any kind of flash. Five to ten metres would be the kind of distance within which accuracy could be controlled. Wind effect would be non-existent. All the same, it was hardly a serious murder weapon.

Unless . . .

The angle from which the scene had been filmed made it impossible to calculate precisely where the gun had been aimed. All that could be said for certain was that from the tilt of the barrel any shot had to hit somebody in the front row; it might have been aimed at any one of the group seated in the middle.

Releasing the still frame button before the shop owner had time to register what he was looking at, Monsieur Pamplemousse re-ran the sequence where the parrot took off. It was impossible to tell exactly what had caused it to panic. The noise of the crowd? Possibly.

Pommes Frites' sudden lunge? That, too, was a possibility.

The squawk it uttered before it fell was barely audible above the sound of cheering.

Perhaps it had simply been a case of some sixth sense warning the bird of impending danger. Once again, for the moment at least, the point was academic.

The plain inescapable fact was that someone disguised as a nun had fired a gun at a member of the audience and by a million to one chance the

184

parrot had got in the way. One bird's misfortune was someone else's good luck. The 64,000 dollar, three in one question was: who fired the shot, at whom and why? The answer to any one of them would help answer the other two.

'Would *Monsieur* like to see the tape again from the start? There is no extra charge.'

Clearly the shop owner was getting more and more intrigued with the whole thing.

'*S'il vous plaît.*' Monsieur Pamplemousse waited while the tape was being rewound. He hadn't the least idea what he was looking for, but it struck him that he might as well get his 400 francs worth while he had the chance.

As the man set the video machine running again Monsieur Pamplemousse gave a start. He had totally forgotten the footage at the beginning of the tape. The forest he had registered on first viewing the tape looked totally different blown up and reproduced in full colour.

White trees metamorphosed into undulating limbs patently made of flesh and blood. That someone was doing something to someone else was obvious, but quite what was hard to say. The picture was distorted through the use of a wide-angle lens in extreme close-up. Much of it was going in and out of focus, and for the same reason the sound, although it came and went, at times sounding like a gale force wind, was clearly brought about by heavy breathing in close proximity to the camera's built-in microphone.

A large cigar seemed to play an important part in the proceedings, for the glowing end appeared from time to time as smoke billowed forth from most unlikely places.

For 'someone in communications', thought Monsieur Pamplemousse, read 'porno movies'. You could argue that it was communication of a sort.

By now thoroughly roused from his post-prandial torpor, the shopkeeper reached for the remote controller. As he turned up the brightness he looked back over his shoulder.

'I am a non-smoker,' said Monsieur Pamplemousse, anticipating the question.

Having denied his role as performer, it struck him that he might well be under suspicion of having operated the camera. He wondered about Abeille. From his limited observation he could vouch for the fact that she wasn't playing a starring role in the picture.

Crouching down in front of the video player, he overrode the remote control by pressing the STOP button, followed by EJECT. As the cassette popped out he quickly withdrew it before the shop owner had time to stop him. He looked the kind of person who might try and confiscate the tape for his own purposes.

'Perhaps *Monsieur* would like to view it again in

comfort?' Sweaty hands resumed their washing in invisible soap mode.

'*Non*,' said Monsieur Pamplemousse. 'I have seen enough.'

'I run a copying service in the back room, *Monsieur*. It is possible we could do a deal. There are other things which might interest you. I have a selection of films and there is a private viewing theatre.'

'*Non*,' repeated Monsieur Pamplemousse firmly.

Having removed the miniature cassette from its holder, he reached inside his cape and slipped it into his trouser leg pocket alongside the notebook and the envelope Fabrice had given him.

Looking the other straight in the eye, he held up the empty adapter. 'Would you be interested in buying one of these?' he enquired. 'Mint condition. Used once only.'

The man shook his head. 'There is no call for them.'

'That is a pity,' said Monsieur Pamplemousse. 'I was hoping I might persuade the police to take a lenient view of your duplicating facilities when I talk to them. Alas . . .'

Four one hundred franc notes appeared as if by magic from the till. The man laid them on the counter as though hardly trusting himself to hand them over personally.

'Next time *Monsieur* wishes to view such films I suggest he buys his own equipment.'

Out of the corner of his eye Monsieur Pamplemousse

caught sight of a woman with a small child sheltering in the doorway. There were two patches of steam on the glass; one above the other. The child asked a question and received a clip round the ear for its pains.

'And I suggest, *Monsieur,* that next time you wish to show such films in your shop you make sure the blinds are drawn, otherwise you may find yourself in trouble under the corruption of minors section of the *Code Civile.*'

Closing the door behind him with a satisfactory bang, Monsieur Pamplemousse nodded a brief apology to the woman and made his way across the deserted *place.* He felt three pairs of eyes boring into his back. If the truth be known, there were probably others as well. Doubtless half the village had viewed the tape via cracks in blinds and shutters. And if they hadn't, word would soon get around. It was the kind of place where very little would pass unnoticed. The bush telegraph would be busy.

As he entered *Paris Modes* (Madame Blanc: Prop. – late of Paris and Rome) his heart sank. Madame Blanc was not far short of being a mirror image of the man he had just left. Only the clothes and the unhappy addition of some lipstick on her front teeth distinguished the one from the other. They had to be brother and sister. Monsieur Pamplemousse wondered if they shared the same stone at night.

Between them they probably had the whole village tied up; a captive market forced to pay over the odds for anything that was needed.

Having exchanged minimal pleasantries he stifled his repugnance and grasped the nettle with both hands. 'I am in need of some clothing . . . ladies clothing.'

Madame Blanc made a show of peering out of the window as though looking for someone.

'*Madame* has had a puncture?'

Monsieur Pamplemousse shook his head. 'I am on my own.'

'Aah!' Madame Blanc understood at once. She was used to dealing with gentlemen customers who wanted to surprise their wives.

'It is for *Madame's anniversaire*?'

'*Non*,' said Monsieur Pamplemousse. 'It is not.' He almost added that he had no wish to fill in a questionnaire on the subject, but waited instead while the problem was considered and evaluated.

'Then *Monsieur* is looking for something a little more general? A souvenir of the area, perhaps? A local costume?'

Monsieur Pamplemousse began to wish he had thought the conversation through beforehand instead of plunging straight in. He tried to remember what Abeille had been wearing. Apart from the négligée, not a lot. Common sense told him it would be as well to get something as near to the original as possible,

189

but looking around the shop he could see nothing remotely resembling any of it.

'Some nightwear,' he said vaguely. 'Of the sort which can also be used during the day.'

'*Quelle age* is *Monsieur*'s wife?'

'A little younger than myself, give or take.' Monsieur Pamplemousse oscillated his free hand up and down in a non-committal fashion, leaving as much latitude as possible.

The proprietress waddled to the other side of the shop and removed a garment from a rail. Breathing heavily from the effort, she returned and spread what looked like the prototype for an early bell tent across the counter. All it needed were some guy ropes.

Monsieur Pamplemousse decided it was time he adopted a more positive approach. 'I am sure it is *très pratique*,' he said tactfully. 'However, my wife is fortunate. She has the figure of a *jeune fille*. A *jeune fille* of, perhaps, twenty-one.'

'*Oooh, là là!*' Madame Blanc wagged a finger at him. 'It sounds as though it is *Monsieur* who is the fortunate one.'

Eyeing Monsieur Pamplemousse with more than passing interest, she moistened her lips with a furry tongue, managing to transfer yet more lipstick to her front teeth in the process.

'*Monsieur* has something "special" in mind?'

'*Comme ci, comme ça.*' Momentarily bereft of

his powers of description, Monsieur Pamplemousse sought refuge in a series of whistles.

It had the desired effect. A gleam came into Madame Blanc's eye as she disappeared into the back room. He caught a brief glimpse of some emergency facial repair work being carried out behind a cupboard door before she returned carrying a large cardboard box, her blood-red lips pursed in what was presumably intended to be an enticing bee-sting smile.

Rummaging inside the box, she discarded some soiled-looking tissue paper, then withdrew the item she had been looking for, holding it up against her ample bosom by way of demonstration.

'This is the number one favourite in the village, *Monsieur*.'

Monsieur Pamplemousse stared at the garment for a moment or two, trying to decide what was meant to go where. The last time he had seen anything similar had been in a shop in the Place de Clichy shortly before the Vice Squad moved in. The makers had called it *un gruyère* after the cheese.

'But it is full of holes!'

Madame Blanc gave a wink. 'That is why it is so popular, *Monsieur*.'

Reaching into the box she withdrew another, smaller piece of frippery, the purpose of which was even harder to imagine, if indeed it had a purpose.

'Should *Madame* suffer from the cold you can always buy her the optional extras.'

Cackling at her own joke, Madame Blanc handed him both garments and reached for the top button of her blouse. 'If *Monsieur* is disposed I can arrange a demonstration.'

Monsieur Pamplemousse reeled slightly both from the thought and from the waft of stale garlic which enveloped him as she attempted to squeeze past. Lingering in the process, Madame Blanc made contact with the snail-filled plastic bag he was still clutching beneath the cape.

'Mon Dieu!' He could feel her hot breath on his face as she crossed herself.

A *FERMÉ* sign in place across the door, she locked it and pointedly dropped the key inside the dark recesses of her cleavage. It disappeared without trace. Beckoning him to follow her, she waddled towards the back room.

'Tell *Madame* we do not do exchanges, but we do have a hire service.'

'You mean . . .' Monsieur Pamplemousse stared after her. 'This has already been worn?'

His remark triggered off a further cackle. 'Not for very long, *Monsieur*. Not for very long.' A blouse landed on the floor at her feet.

Turning her back on him, Madame Blanc began making heavy weather of undoing the straps holding her brassiere in place. The invitation was clear.

Taking advantage of the moment, Monsieur Pamplemousse gazed round the shop. The choice, if it could be called a choice, lay between retrieving the key – and he doubted if even Madame Blanc herself knew where it had ended up – or making good his escape. Desperate situations demanded desperate measures.

He was in the process of trying to gauge the age and thickness of the door, recalling times past when one well-aimed kick with all his weight behind it had usually done the trick, wondering if old skills learnt in the *Sûreté* might come to his aid, when he heard the telephone ring.

It triggered off a muffled exclamation.

While Madame Blanc took the call, he crossed to the window and lifted the blind to make sure his *bicyclette* was still where he had left it. On the other side of the *place* he could see the owner of *Videos Extraordinaires* behind his counter. He was holding a receiver to his ear. Lip movements coincided with gaps in the conversation at his end.

Turning away from the window, Monsieur Pamplemousse was just in time to see Madame Blanc push the connecting door partly closed with the heel of her shoe. If he'd had any doubts about the reason for the call, he dismissed them. Her voice had taken on a different tone. A shadow fell across the opening as she retrieved her blouse.

It was now or never and the decision was no

longer in doubt. Counting out what seemed to be a reasonable sum of money in view of the paucity of material, Monsieur Pamplemousse stuffed the garments into his trouser pocket.

He was in the act of bracing himself when he recalled the other Shakespearean quotation he had learnt as a boy. 'Hell hath no fury like a woman scorned'.

Who knew what sort of story Madame Blanc might concoct to wreak her revenge? Too bad. Whatever she dreamt up it couldn't make his current situation any worse.

Stay, and he might well risk being accused of attempted rape, or worse. Go, and for the time being at least he would remain master of his own destiny.

Monsieur Pamplemousse felt sure that had he found himself in a similar situation, Shakespeare would have reached very much the same conclusion. He might even have dreamt up a suitable quotation as he put his boot through the door.

The same might equally well have been said, albeit in a different context, about Pommes Frites. Had he been waylaid in the street by someone with a clipboard carrying out a nationwide survey on the likes and dislikes of the canine population of France he would unhesitatingly have placed his 'likes' tick in the section set aside for those *chiens* who were of an urban disposition. And had that happened he would undoubtedly have added a suitable crisp quotation on the shortcomings of the countryside in general for good measure.

If pushed to award marks, he would have given the countryside perhaps three out of ten, as against a maximum ten out of ten for somewhere like Paris, pointing to the fact that in the country it was sometimes possible to go for hours on end without anything happening at all, especially when it was raining. Then, as often as not, when something did occur you were so taken by surprise that the chances were you missed it altogether.

One quick blink in order to make sure you weren't dreaming and by the time you opened your eyes again what you thought you had seen was no longer there.

Pommes Frites could have filled a multi-paged questionnaire on the subject in no time at all.

The present occasion was a good example, and it wasn't helped by the restricted view through the porthole of his master's cabin. By standing on the bed he could just about see one half of the bridge spanning the canal at Bussière-sur-Ouche, together with a short section of the road leading to it, but no more.

What he thought he saw – and it had been just a momentary glimpse, no more – was his master shooting across the canal on a *bicyclette*; head down, cape flying in the wind, as though his very life depended on it. Pommes Frites barely had time to take in the fact, when Monsieur Pamplemousse reappeared, this time heading in the opposite direction. He skidded to a stop, fell off his machine, then lifted it high above his head as though about to throw it in the canal.

It was then, when Pommes Frites' powers of absorption felt as though they had reached saturation point, that he closed his eyes.

When he opened them again he found to his surprise that the scene had completely changed. Both master and *bicyclette* had vanished and their place had been taken by a police car and two *gendarmes*, both of whom were scanning the canal bank on either side of the bridge, obviously as mystified as he was.

Pommes Frites' opinion of the countryside in general and portholes in particular reached a new low. One way and another he'd had his fill of both for one day. Had he been writing to a local *journal* he would have signed himself 'Disgusted of Paris'. It would have boded ill for any researcher wanting to pursue the subject to the bitter end.

One thing was abundantly clear. His master was in trouble and it was time for action.

In a matter of seconds Pommes Frites was on the towpath and racing towards the bridge. With what to some might have seemed an uncanny show of cunning, but to one who had received his training in the *chiens* section of the Paris *Sûreté* was all in a day's work, he timed to perfection the moment when both policemen had their backs to him. Racing across the road, he leapt over a ditch and into a field. Once there he gave voice to a blood-curdling mixture of baying and snarling, coupled with leaps and bounds, as though engaged in doing battle with an assailant of the very worst kind. Rin Tin Tin at the height of his powers could have done no better, and even then he would have needed a good many retakes to get his timing right.

Glancing briefly over his shoulder as he sped through the sodden grass, he saw to his satisfaction that his ruse had worked. The two *gendarmes* were engaged in hot pursuit. It was now only a matter of leading them as far away from the boat as possible before giving them the slip so that he could return to the bridge.

In the event the reunion of master and hound was necessarily brief. Marcel Carné would have milked the Simenon-like scenario to the full, making much of the canal, the remorseless rain, and of Monsieur Pamplemousse hiding under the bridge. Art cinemas the world over would have treasured for years to come the moment when Pommes Frites caught sight of his master and stopped dead in his tracks.

But there was no time to lose. Greetings exchanged, and having made certain the coast was clear, they set off as fast as they could go along the towpath towards *Le Creuset*, each basking in the sheer pleasure of the other's company, both busy with their own thoughts.

In one sense it was communication at the highest level; speech was rendered totally redundant.

Not for Pommes Frites the human error of assuming that things said necessarily conveyed the meaning the speaker intended, and in Monsieur Pamplemousse's case so much had happened in such a short space of time he would have been hard put to condense it into words anyway.

It would be impossible to explain to Pommes Frites, *par exemple*, that the reason why he was walking with a limp was because the door to *Paris Modes* (Madame Blanc: Prop.) had proved unexpectedly resistant to being kicked open. Nor, for the moment, could he have given a lucid blow by blow account of his nightmare ride down the steeply winding hill leading to the Vallée d'Ouche.

On his part, Pommes Frites wondered if his master really thought he had been stuck in the porthole a second time. Once had been quite enough. No self-respecting dog would let it happen twice.

Clearly his master hadn't wanted his, Pommes Frites', face to be seen, otherwise why would he have covered it with his trousers? Therefore it had been a case of doing the right thing and pretending to be stuck. But that, in turn, could mean only one thing; Monsieur Pamplemousse must know what Pommes Frites knew. But did he know that Pommes Frites knew that he knew what he knew? And if he did, then why hadn't he done something about it? It was a puzzle and no mistake.

As they drew near to *Le Creuset* Pommes Frites wondered if he should give a demonstration of his command of portholes, but glancing up at his master, he felt less than reassured; he clearly had his mind on other things.

Unaware of the thought processes going on alongside him, Monsieur Pamplemousse took stock of the situation. Everything was quiet. The fact that the coach was nowhere to be seen suggested an outing was taking place, which meant the rest of the crew would be taking it easy. It would be sensible to make sure Pommes Frites wasn't seen by the police. If he were and they connected him to *Le Creuset* the two *gendarmes* would be on to him like a shot.

He decided to take a chance. Explanations could come later if need be. Signalling Pommes Frites to follow on behind, Monsieur Pamplemousse made his way up the gangplank.

He braced himself as he reached his cabin. Expecting the home-made wedge to be still in place he knocked on the door and to his surprise it swung open, revealing an empty room.

Removing his cape, Monsieur Pamplemousse registered Abeille's absence with a sense of shock. It was the last thing he had expected. He felt the bed. There was a hollow just below the porthole where she must have sat awaiting his return. It was still warm to the touch, so it couldn't be that long since she had left. He wondered whether to go looking for her, but decided against it. Perhaps someone else had come to the rescue. Boniface? There would be hell to pay if that were the case.

Contemplating his next move, going back over things in his mind, Monsieur Pamplemousse suddenly remembered the *escargots*. There had been a moment during his flight down the hill when he had almost collided with a vanload of police going in the opposite direction and he'd literally had to throw himself off the *bicyclette* into the bushes. Fortunately the van had been going so fast the attention of those inside had been focused on the road ahead. Only two dogs gazing mournfully out of the back window had registered his presence. It was too bad the bag had burst when he landed. Never mind. He knew where they were. Perhaps he could return later.

The loss of the *escargots* reminded him of the envelope Fabrice Delamain had given him. He felt in his pocket. It was still there.

Ripping it open, he emptied the contents on to the dressing table.

Several bloodstained feathers fell out, along with a small air gun pellet. The pellet looked as though it had started off as a 0.22 hollow point. There was the familiar mushroom shape to the head where it had expanded on impact, producing added shock effect, but the hollow was still visible. In its original form it would have been large enough to have been laced with a few grains of cyanide, or some other poisonous substance like Ricin, sealed in place by a dab of paraffin wax.

If that were so, what might have been intended simply as a warning shot, became a serious attempt at murder.

Murder would be hard to prove had either been used. Ricin was a natural toxin – one of the most powerful in the world. Extracted from the castor bean plant, it had double the toxicity of cobra venom, as the defecting Bulgarian agent Georgi Markov had found to his cost via a jab from an umbrella tip on the London underground. In India it was known as 'mother-in-law's poison' because of its ability to kill without producing any obvious symptoms.

With cyanide the victim became unconscious almost immediately. Death could take place within one to fifteen minutes; the fastest ever recorded was ten seconds.

The classic symptoms were for the victim to turn reddish blue in the face, but who would ever know with a parrot?

Monsieur Pamplemousse placed the pellet and the feather carefully inside his wallet.

One thing was certain: Pommes Frites had had a lucky escape. A less well-trained hound might well have treated Vert-Vert as manna from heaven and devoured it on the spot.

Signalling Pommes Frites to make room, he lay back on the bed in order to consider the matter. As he did so he felt a lump underneath the bedclothes.

It was the book Abeille had been reading. If the title *For the Love of Lilies* wasn't exactly memorable, he recognised the dust jacket immediately and he was about to toss it to one side when something made him look inside.

To his surprise the contents bore little relation to the lurid cover, which showed the body of a scantily-clad girl floating face upwards in a pond. It was an English paperback edition of *Every Secret Thing* by Patty Hearst; the story of the Californian heiress's kidnapping by an urban terrorist organisation who called themselves the Symbionese Liberation Army. According to the blurb there had been a film of the story with Natasha Richardson in the leading role, but he didn't recall seeing it at the time.

It was a reversal of the normal turn of events; a relatively serious book being passed off as a pulp novel.

Monsieur Pamplemousse stared at it. Riffling through the five hundred or so pages, he came across several slips of paper inserted at intervals along with an occasional pencilled exclamation mark in the margin, but the print was small and the effort of translating the relevant passages was not something he felt in the mood to attempt until he'd had a chance to recover from his ordeal.

But why conceal the book with another dust jacket? It was hardly banned material. And who was she hiding it from? Only Abeille could answer that question, and for the moment at least, for all he knew she could be on the other side of the moon.

CHAPTER EIGHT

Monsieur Pamplemousse woke the next morning to find the sun streaming in through the porthole above his bed. Reaching out, he felt for his watch. It showed a few minutes past seven-thirty. He must have slept like the proverbial log. They both had. Curled up in the middle of the floor, Pommes Frites looked as though he hadn't moved so much as a whisker all night.

It was a moment or two before Monsieur Pamplemousse could summon the energy to struggle into a sitting position. Muscles he had almost forgotten he possessed acted as an aching reminder of all that had taken place the previous day and eventually spurred him into action.

He took a look at the view outside. It was a glorious day. Overnight the clouds had completely disappeared; almost as though a blanket had been rolled back. A thin layer of ground mist still covered pockets in the low-lying areas, but in another hour or so it would be gone.

The coach was parked near the lock. He'd heard it arrive back late the previous evening. Otherwise the only sign of life came from a little way beyond the bridge, where another barge was moored; a thin wisp of blue smoke rose from the chimney above its galley.

Having washed, shaved and sponged the worst of the mud from his suit, Monsieur Pamplemousse led the way up on deck, ready to face the world.

None of the crew were around and a notice on the board near the bar proclaimed a 'free day'. The wording made it sound like an act of benevolence on the part of the tour company. Certainly the rest of the passengers seemed to be taking full advantage of it.

A flotilla of ducks zigzagged past the boat, heading towards the lock. Finding the gates at the far end closed, they turned and set off on the return journey. A line of multi-coloured statuary, gnomes, donkeys, and other fauna watched over them with dispassionate eyes. The windows of the lock-keeper's cottage were still shuttered, a reminder, if one were needed, that it was Sunday.

The peace was short-lived. A grey van drew up, parked just short of the bridge, and an elderly *gendarme* climbed out. He went round the back to open the doors, and six men in wetsuits emerged. They padded across to the lock and peered over the side. The leader flipped open a walkie-talkie and began a conversation with someone.

Monsieur Pamplemousse hesitated, torn between wanting to see what was going on and taking *petit déjeuner*. Having gone without a meal the previous evening, breakfast won.

Returning Pommes Frites to the cabin, he bade him await his return and made his way up to the saloon.

The long serving table was already prepared. A basket of bread, another of *pain d'épice* – the local spiced honeycake – bowls of *confiture, croissants, brioche,* ham, cheese, fruit. He helped himself to a selection, putting a generous portion of ham on another plate for Pommes Frites.

Monique's face appeared behind a window let into the galley door.

Monsieur Pamplemousse mimed fruit juice and *café* at her. She waved acknowledgement of the order and disappeared.

Glancing at the books on the library shelves while he awaited their arrival, he spotted the missing book. Deprived of its jacket, it looked as anonymous as those on either side; the title made it sound like a volume on gardening.

It wasn't until he sat down that it crossed Monsieur Pamplemousse's mind to wonder how

Abeille had got hold of her book in the first place. He was sure it hadn't been in his cabin when he arrived, and equally certain she hadn't been carrying it when she brought the tape to show him. She could hardly have been up to the saloon while the lecture was in progress. The obvious inference was that during the short time he'd been away she had returned to her own quarters to fetch it. But if that was so, what had happened to JayCee? Unless, of course, he had fallen asleep again. Pommes Frites probably knew the answer, but that was no help.

Café and a large glass of freshly squeezed *jus d'orange* appeared at his table. There was also a message for him to telephone the Director as soon as he could.

'When did this arrive?'

'Yesterday evening. Boniface was given it at the hotel in Dijon where the party was being held. It was late when he got back and we thought it best not to disturb you.'

Monsieur Pamplemousse nodded. The Director must have thought the matter urgent if he had spent his Saturday evening tracking down *Le Creuset*'s comings and goings.

'*Monsieur* is up early.' Monique noticed the extra plate of ham and brought him a knife and fork.

Monsieur Pamplemousse pretended to toy with them. 'It is the best part of the day.'

'*Bien dormi?*'

'*Oui, merci.* Where is everybody?'

Monique made a steeple of her hands. Resting her head on the side, she pulled a face. 'Sleeping it off. There was a big tasting in Beaune last night.'

As the door to the galley shut behind her he heard footsteps on the stairs.

'*Bonjour.*' It was Colonel Massingham.

Monsieur Pamplemousse's heart sank. He was in no mood for an early morning lecture, whatever the subject.

But Colonel Massingham seemed unusually subdued. He browsed amongst the *croissants* for a while before returning.

'Mind if I join you?'

'Please.' It would have sounded churlish not to say yes.

'Didn't see you at the do last night.'

'I was catching up on my sleep.'

'Can't say I blame you. Guess what we had to eat?'

'*Jambon persillé?*'

'And *boeuf Bourgignon*,' said the Colonel gloomily. 'There were two other coachloads. They'd been at it all day. The "twelve hour special". Ten wine tastings, followed by a "gourmet" dinner. There was a ghastly sing-song afterwards.'

Monsieur Pamplemousse reflected that Madame Ambert was right. Either you were a serious wine-maker or you were in the entertainment business. The two didn't mix.

Colonel Massingham broke a *croissant* in half, eyeing the two ends with approval.

'Can't get them like this in England. Not the same. Not buttery enough. Give you indigestion.'

'It is getting more difficult in France,' said Monsieur Pamplemousse. 'True *croissants* belong to a more leisurely age. Making them requires time and dedication. Two factors which are in increasingly short supply.'

'Same with the jam,' said Colonel Massingham. 'Only got to read the list of contents on the jar. "E" this, "E" that. Gelling agents, colouring agents, emulsion stabilisers, artificial sweeteners, preservatives – bit of a joke that, adding preservatives to preserves. Went round a jam factory once. Never again . . .'

'Try this.' Monsieur Pamplemousse hastily pushed a bowl of *confiture* across the table before the other got into his stride. 'Fruit, sugar, natural pectin . . .'

'*Merci*.' Colonel Massingham hesitated. 'Changing the subject. Haven't thanked you for letting me take over yesterday. It was most enjoyable.'

'You did me a favour,' said Monsieur Pamplemousse.

'Not as big as the one you did me. Don't know quite how to say this, old boy, but thanks. And thanks for the other, too . . .'

Monsieur Pamplemousse stared at Colonel Massingham for a moment, wondering what he was about to say.

'Tell you the truth, Mrs Massingham can be a bit demandin' at times. Thinks of nothing else.'

'She has told you?'

'She always tells me,' said Colonel Massingham simply. 'And shell go on telling me until the next one. It's like a drippin' tap.'

Monsieur Pamplemousse had a momentary picture of wasted lives. An arid desert inhabited by two people making the best of things, yet in one case at least, dreaming of an escape that would never happen; a voice crying out in the wilderness. Physically together, yet suffering the most dreadful poverty of all, that of loneliness. One never really knew what went on behind the closed shutters of other people's lives.

'I shall not tell anyone,' he said.

'Thanks, old boy. Do the same for you if I could.'

'With respect,' said Monsieur Pamplemousse dryly, 'I like to think that Madame Pamplemousse would not necessarily thank you.'

'Ha! Good point that!' Colonel Massingham chuckled at the idea.

They ate in silence for a while. It seemed to Monsieur Pamplemousse that there was more to come, if that were possible.

'Tell you what, though.' Colonel Massingham was the first to speak. 'One good turn deserves another. You know that gal you've been knocking about with. Miss Gridlock I call her.

'Thought you two were up to no good at one time, until Mabel told me what she told me. Anyway, the thing is, she's not what she seems. Neither is he for that matter. For a start, the newspaper he says he owns doesn't exist. I got that from one of the other Americans. They were all talking about it the other evening. Couple of phonies if you ask me. Thought I ought to warn you.'

It came as no great surprise, but Monsieur Pamplemousse thanked him all the same. He wondered what the Colonel would think if he knew about the tape. It would confirm his worst suspicions.

'Not that it matters much. Don't suppose we shall ever see them again.'

Monsieur Pamplemousse sat up, suddenly alert.

'I do not understand. How is that?'

'They left yesterday afternoon. Gone to stay in Beaune according to Boniface. Hôtel le Cep. Good place. Stayed there once myself.'

Catching sight of a figure hovering on the other side of the galley door, Monsieur Pamplemousse dabbed at his mouth with a napkin and rose from the table. It looked as though Monique was about to bring in the Colonel's coffee. If he wasn't careful she would clear the table of Pommes Frites' breakfast as well. He picked up the plate.

'Please forgive me, *Monsieur*.'

Colonel Massingham stood and held out his hand.

'Of course. Glad to have had the opportunity of a chat. Clear the air a bit.'

Monsieur Pamplemousse shook hands absent-mindedly. He had just remembered something about Patty Hearst and the Symbionese Liberation Army.

Back in his cabin, and Pommes Frites' immediate needs catered for, he returned to the first of several marked paragraphs in Abeille's book. It contained a detailed description of how the gang had made up special shells – 00 buckshot laced with 'Ajax' – their code name for cyanide – for use in sawn-off shot guns. For 00 buckshot read air gun slug. Another paragraph dealt with the drilling out of lead bullets. He wondered who had done the marking, JayCee or Abeille?

Leaving Pommes Frites to carry on with his breakfast, Monsieur Pamplemousse made his way off the boat in search of a telephone. His cabin had yet to be made up, but he would have to take a chance on it happening. Being a Sunday he was probably safe for a while.

A television crew had arrived and were busy setting up their cameras. A girl in a zip-fronted red nylon wind-cheater and designer jeans took a quick look at herself in a mirror and began rehearsing her lines into a microphone. The lock-keeper and his wife had emerged from their cottage to keep a watchful eye on their territory.

Monsieur Pamplemousse approached the *gendarme* he had seen earlier.

'*M'sieur*.' He nodded towards the lock. 'You have problems?'

'*Oui!*' The man saluted, then turned away.

Sensing that he wasn't going to get very far by the direct route, Monsieur Pamplemousse tried another tack.

'Is Lobinière still with you?' He mentioned a colleague from long ago who had since risen to dizzy heights in the area. It had the desired effect.

'Lobinière? You know him?'

'Knew,' said Monsieur Pamplemousse. 'We worked together for many years.'

The man shook his head sadly. 'He retired last year. His replacement is from the cradle!' Raising his eyes to heaven, he held his right hand out, palm down, to indicate extreme youth. 'Wet behind the ears.'

'*Alors!*' Monsieur Pamplemousse made sympathetic noises. 'He will get over it. It is the same in Paris. The *Sûreté* is not what it was. They get younger every day.'

He was home and dry. A bond had been established. It was time for the big one.

'I am in need of a telephone,' he said casually. 'I have an urgent call to make.'

The *gendarme* looked around to make sure the others were all busy, then he beckoned Monsieur Pamplemousse to follow him back to the van.

'It is all yours . . .' He pointed to a receiver under the dashboard. 'Make sure you put it back properly or I shall be in trouble.'

He hovered for a moment while Monsieur Pamplemousse made himself comfortable. 'Have we met before?'

'I think not,' said Monsieur Pamplemousse. 'It is possible you may have seen my photograph.' There had been a time when never a week went by without his picture appearing in one *journal* or another. It still followed him around.

The Director must have been either waiting by the phone or still in bed, for he lost no time in coming to the point.

'Where are you, Pamplemousse? I tried in vain to call you last night. No one knew where you were.'

'I am in a police van, *Monsieur.*'

'Not bad news I trust?'

'No, *Monsieur.* Expediency.'

'Good. Good. *Excellent,* in fact.' The Director sounded genuinely relieved. 'Things always seem worse at night, but yesterday evening when we were going to bed Chantal and I had sudden fears for your safety. We pictured you being taken unaware on some lonely towpath whilst walking off the effects of one of those *gourmet* meals depicted in the brochure . . . unable to call on Pommes Frites for assistance owing to his being in a weakened condition as a result of the strict *régime* . . .'

215

Monsieur Pamplemousse stared at the telephone, trying hard to picture Monsieur Leclercq and his wife discussing his possible plight while they were retiring for the night. It was yet another example of not knowing what went on behind the closed doors of people one thought one knew; what flights of fancy they indulged in.

'It is kind of you, *Monsieur*. I am deeply touched, and I am sure Pommes Frites would be too, but may I ask why such thoughts entered your heads?'

'Have you not heard?' The Director sounded equally amazed. 'It was on all the bulletins yesterday evening. Channel Two overran and I had to adjust the automatic timing device on my recorder for the start of a late night film.'

'One becomes very detached from bulletins when afloat, *Monsieur*. It is like being in another world.'

'In that case I will bring you up to date. There is a madman loose in your area; a sex maniac of the very worst kind. A serial underwear fetishist who clearly will stop at nothing in order to satisfy his evil cravings. Articles of intimate female attire have been found strewn along the banks of the Canal de Bourgogne – sometimes in the reeds, at other times hanging from trees. The search for bodies goes on.'

'Bodies, *Monsieur*? But . . .'

'Bodies, Pamplemousse. So far they have been unsuccessful, but they are putting every available man on the job.

'That is why you must take care. Who knows how he will react if he finds himself cornered?'

Catching sight of the *gendarme* glancing in his direction, Monsieur Pamplemousse pulled his hat down over his forehead and sank below the level of the windscreen. 'Do they have a description, *Monsieur*?'

'Just an artist's impression, and you know only too well what they can be like. It was provided by the owner of a village shop who narrowly escaped death or even worse . . .'

'Worse than death, *Monsieur*?'

'Old fashioned as it may sound, Pamplemousse,' said the Director severely, 'there are still those who can picture a fate worse than death.

'The poor girl was forcibly detained on the premises while articles of clothing were removed.'

'From her person, *Monsieur*? That is monstrous.'

'No, no, Pamplemousse. From the counter, along with the entire contents of the till. Apparently it was the day for going to the bank, so there was a considerable sum.

'One of the stolen items was found last night floating in a lock near where I believe *Le Creuset* is moored.'

Monsieur Pamplemousse drew in his breath. It must have fallen out of his pocket when he was hiding under the bridge. He peered over the top of the dashboard. Boniface had arrived on the scene

217

and was half-heartedly cleaning his windscreen, trying to chat up the girl with the microphone at the same time. It didn't look as though he was getting very far.

'According to the girl's description,' continued the Director, 'he was an unsavoury character, with staring eyes and slobber all down his chin.'

And that is just in black and white, thought Monsieur Pamplemousse. Wait until *Ici Paris* does it in colour. Madame Blanc was certainly getting her own back.

'What else is this man supposed to have done?' he asked.

'Things that can only be expressed by innuendo,' replied the Director. 'Apparently he could hardly keep his hands off her. The poor girl had to take refuge in the back room. She is too distressed to give any more details for the time being.

'In the meantime there has been a strange turn of events in some nearby woods – the Fôret Dom de Detain-Gerguil. Two sniffer dogs picked up the scent of her assailant and while they were hot on the trail they made an extraordinary discovery. You will never guess what it is.'

'Tell me, *Monsieur*,' said Monsieur Pamplemousse wearily. It was too early in the morning for guessing games, especially when he was assailed by a dreadful feeling that everything was closing in around him.

'*Escargots* have been found, Pamplemousse; in an

area where none have ever been seen before. One of the dogs went into the woods, not once but several times, and on each occasion it returned with a fresh one in its mouth! Furthermore they have been identified as the genuine article – *helix pomotia.*

'The theory is they have moved north to higher ground to escape the worst of the weather.'

'It is a long way for an *escargot* to walk, *Monsieur.*'

'Not if they were desperate, Pamplemousse. It is, I believe, an omen of some kind.

'Already it is being compared to the miracle of the loaves and the fishes. The police are keeping the exact location a secret, of course . . . but naturally the main purpose of the search has temporarily ground to a halt.

'The President has been informed . . .'

Monsieur Pamplemousse felt his head starting to swim as the enormity of the situation sank in. Reaching for a handkerchief he began mopping his brow. Out of the corner of his eye he caught sight of the *gendarme* staring at him and realised to his horror that the 'handkerchief' he was using had a lace edge to it. He hastily replaced the article inside his pocket.

'That is terrible, *Monsieur.* He must be disinformed as soon as possible. There has to be some other explanation. They could have been left behind by someone on a picnic . . .'

'In this weather? I ask you, Pamplemousse, is that likely?'

'Perhaps they are imported?' said Monsieur Pamplemousse desperately.

'Heaven forbid! Black armbands will be worn in Dijon if that is the case.

'But all is not gloom. I have one piece of good news for you. It seems they have established the identity of the man I spoke about yesterday; the one who was found in the wine press. His picture was in this morning's *journaux*. His name is Ponchaud and he is a tax inspector. Apparently he was sent to investigate the peripheral activities of some of the Burgundian wine-makers. The tie-in between vineyards and other enterprises in the world of travel was high on his list. Money changing hands in return for services rendered. Tour companies have their favourite stopping places . . . palms are greased.

'He was found prowling on Madame Ambert's estate and some of the workers decided to teach him a lesson. They plead innocence, of course, saying they thought he was a common or garden thief. I have my doubts, but it will be hard to prove otherwise.

'There is a picture of him in a hospital bed. A rather pathetic figure. According to the report he couldn't justify his expenses taking the trip on your boat so he tagged along on foot. His catchphrase "I mingle, then, when the moment is right, I pounce" has a hollow ring to it now. He pounced once too often and in the wrong place.'

'He was lucky he had a strong suitcase with him,'

said Monsieur Pamplemousse. 'They might have given the screw an extra half turn for luck.'

'You will never guess what was inside it,' said the Director.

'Some half-eaten sandwiches . . . a *pomme* . . . some *journaux* . . . a camera . . . ?' hazarded Monsieur Pamplemousse.

There was a long pause. 'You really are an incredible *homme,* Aristide,' said the Director. 'It is no wonder I turn to you on occasions like this.'

Monsieur Pamplemousse felt better. Four out of four wasn't bad. Perhaps his luck was changing.

'I gather you have seen my aunt.'

'I shall be seeing her again shortly, *Monsieur.*'

'Good. She sounded somewhat down when I spoke to her yesterday evening; in need of counsel. The whole business with Ponchaud has upset her. The very thought of being under suspicion in that way is alien to her way of doing things. I will tell Chantal. She will be pleased. In the meantime, Aristide, take great care. We cannot afford to lose you. Let us hope the fiend is soon caught.'

'I think I may say, *Monsieur,*' said Monsieur Pamplemousse, 'that I am as safe from his attentions as anyone.'

As he hung up he caught sight of the girl with the microphone. She was interviewing one of the divers. He was holding a dripping bicycle.

Retrieving the card Madame Ambert had given

him, Monsieur Pamplemousse dialled the number.

It was some while before anyone answered and when they did it was an unfamiliar male voice.

'Tell Madame Ambert I will be with her as soon as possible.' He gave his name, then hung up before any offers were made to collect him.

Luckily the portion of deck where the bicycles were stored was facing away from the lock, but it could only be a matter of time before the police put two and two together and equated the trail of scattered lingerie with the movement of Le *Creuset*. The question of the snails was at best only a temporary diversion. Now was probably as good a time as any to put as much distance as possible between himself and the boat.

Making his way to the coach Monsieur Pamplemousse approached Boniface. 'Would you care,' he said, feeling for his wallet, 'to do Pommes Frites and myself a very great favour on your day off?'

Boniface waited until they reached Sainte-Marie-sur-Ouche, some ten or twelve kilometres back down the canal, before cutting across the mountains in the direction of Gevrey-Chambertin. There had been a bad moment soon after they set off when Monsieur Pamplemousse thought they were going to travel via the road he had cycled down the day before, but there was a *ROUTE BARRÉE* notice at the junction. A *gendarme* waved them back. The Director had been right about the *escargots* being taken seriously.

Everywhere he looked there were men out with their shotguns at the ready; sometimes in small parties, more often than not alone or with their dogs.

'It is worse in September,' said Boniface. Removing both hands from the steering wheel, he took a pot shot at an imaginary rabbit. 'On the first day of the hunting season it is not safe to be out. People shut themselves in their houses.'

Monsieur Pamplemousse wondered if Boniface had heard the latest news. Quite possibly not. It was a topsy-turvy world where people miles away, sometimes on the other side of the globe, had more up-to-date information than did the people on the spot. He made no mention of the rapist. Topics ranged from the change in the weather to a long saga about his childhood in Italy. It was a relief when they turned off the main road. At least the narrow, winding minor road demanded his full attention. Even Pommes Frites looked relieved to be left in peace.

Their departure from *Le Creuset* had been necessarily abrupt, the explanation perfunctory; an urgent message to return to Paris covered a multitude of sins. At least he'd been spared having to shake hands all round.

Dropping down from the hills, Boniface turned off to the right in Gevrey-Chambertin, following the route they had taken on the very first evening.

Shortly afterwards Clos Ambert-Celeste came into view.

As they drove in through the entrance gates Monsieur Pamplemousse noticed something he had missed on the first occasion. At the end of each row of vines there was a dark red rose bush. He wondered if they were Papa Meilland. It was one of Doucette's favourites.

The planting of rose bushes in a vineyard was an old fashioned conceit, more often seen in Bordeaux or the Rhône valley than in Bourgogne. The origins of the custom were lost in time. Some people maintained it was to stop horses accidentally trampling on the vines when they reached the end of a row, others argued that was nonsense, horses were much too sensible to do any such thing, subscribing instead to the theory that since roses were invariably quicker than vines to show signs of blight or other disease, they acted as Nature's warning. Papa Meilland was certainly prone to mildew; it was one of its few drawbacks.

Whatever the reason, it was pleasant to see old traditions being kept alive, if only as a token gesture. It was typical, too, of Madame Ambert. Her brother would probably be all for grubbing the bushes up on the grounds that they were an unproductive use of the land.

There were vines on either side. They ran parallel

to the long, straight gravelled drive as it led them up a gentle slope towards a grey stone house standing on the brow of the hill. The grapes were starting to fill out and change colour, from green to russet red. In other circumstances he would have dearly liked to stop and take some photographs. Perhaps another time.

Fabrice Delamain's Mercedes was parked in a circular area outside the house and Boniface drew up alongside it. An open garage door revealed two other cars, one of which he recognised as Madame Ambert's. To the right of the house he could see a couple of battered Renaults and a moped, otherwise all was quiet.

Boniface helped him with the luggage and they shook hands.

'Next year, *Monsieur*?'

'*Oui. L'année prochaine.*' Monsieur Pamplemousse repeated the well-worn phrase automatically, but next year was a long way ahead. He doubted if it would happen.

Waving goodbye, he watched the coach disappear back down the driveway, then he turned and, leaving Pommes Frites to watch over the bags, made his way to the front door. It was opened by a man, he presumed the same one who had answered the phone earlier. It felt colder inside than it did outdoors.

Madame Ambert received him in the drawing room. It was furnished in much the same way as the hall, a reflection of the house itself; old, plain and serviceable. The Director's aunt evidently belonged to a stratum of society who lived well but considered creature comforts a sign of weakness and had schooled themselves to do without such things; what had been good enough for their forefathers was good enough for them. The long curtains reaching to the floor were partly drawn, shutting out the sunlight and casting the room in shadow. Even so, as they exchanged a few pleasantries he could see Madame Ambert looked pale. Her eyes were red, as though she had recently been crying.

'It is good of you to come.'

'I am sorry to be late. I'm afraid there were complications.' Monsieur Pamplemousse saw no point in going into details. 'Your brother is with you?'

'You wish to see him?'

'It is partly why I am here.'

'In that case, please follow me.'

Madame Ambert led the way out of the drawing room and along a stone-flagged passage towards the back of the house. Pausing before she opened it, as though gathering strength, she stood back for Monsieur Pamplemousse to enter first.

He found himself in what appeared to be an office cum workroom. There was a large desk under the window, and bookshelves lined the walls. As before, the curtains were drawn and it took him a moment before his eyes grew accustomed to the level of light.

Dominique Ambert was much as he remembered him from the brief encounter on the night of the pageant. A little smaller, perhaps, but that might have been the way he was sitting. He was dressed for a shoot rather than a concert; corduroy trousers and a hunting jacket.

He returned Monsieur Pamplemousse's gaze open-mouthed; his eyes reflecting a mixture of surprise and fear, as well they might, for he had been shot in the head and he was very, very dead.

CHAPTER NINE

It was the hour of the morning *affluence* in Beaune and the *gare* was crowded. Being a Monday, half the people there were wanting a weekly season ticket, which didn't help matters.

Rather than stand in a long line at the ticket office, Monsieur Pamplemousse decided to use one of the new computerised *billetterie automatique* machines.

The fact that all the regulars obviously preferred queuing should have warned him. Doubtless it was all very wonderful; a child of eight would have been in its element. But the person who had designed the machine – and it wasn't long before Monsieur Pamplemousse formed a vivid mental picture of what he must look like: sandals, beard, steel-framed spectacles, an absent-minded air – had clearly never in his life been in a hurry to catch a train. The machine posed so many questions and offered so many alternative replies to each and every one, his mind was soon reeling under the onslaught.

The final insult came when, having at last established beyond a shadow of doubt that, God willing, he had every intention of leaving Beaune that day *en route* to Dijon in a first class compartment, never to return, and that he had no intention of claiming any special status, either as a student or indeed in any of the many categories privileged to enjoy special rates, the machine enquired how he wished to pay. Opting to use his *carte bleu* credit card – one of several options at his disposal – the machine refused to accept it. No reason was given for the rejection, nor did it offer anything in the way of compensation for the loss of his valuable time. A priority voucher for the queue, which by now reached as far as the door, would not have come amiss, but the subject was clearly not up for discussion. The only saving grace was that it didn't actually *mange* his card.

In the end, having watched his abortive efforts with growing impatience, a small boy with glasses and roller skates offered to help him out.

Swallowing his pride, Monsieur Pamplemousse gave him five francs for his trouble – a rate of roughly 300 francs an hour – and managed to scramble aboard the 9.30 train to Dijon seconds before the guard blew his whistle.

The consequence of it all was that not only did he spend the first five minutes of the quarter hour journey recovering both his breath and his temper, but he also failed to register Pommes Frites' strange behaviour.

By the time he did sit up and take notice it was too late. Pommes Frites had given him up as a bad job. Warnings had been issued: if his master didn't wish to take note of them, that was up to him. Perhaps he had good reason for not caring who else was travelling on the train. Perhaps even now, behind the mask of indifference, his master was playing a waiting game. He, Pommes Frites, had done his best. A dog couldn't do more.

Unaware of all that was going on in Pommes Frites' head, Monsieur Pamplemousse was conscious only of a recumbent form curled up on the floor at his feet. That, and an occasional feeling of unease as an eyelid was opened and a reproachful, if bloodshot eye fastened itself on him.

Ignoring it as best he could, he removed a note from his wallet and read it once again. Roughly printed on black ink on a plain sheet of paper, brief and to the point, it requested a meeting in Dijon at ten o'clock that morning. To be exact, a meeting in the crypt of the Cathédral St Bénigne. For whatever reason, the writer of the note must have gone to a lot of trouble to find somewhere where they wouldn't be seen together.

The note had arrived along with his breakfast at eight o'clock. According to the porter at the hotel in Beaune where he had spent the night, someone must have left it on the reception desk earlier that morning when no one else was around.

Monsieur Pamplemousse gazed out of the train window. To his right lay the *autoroute*, crowded in both directions with fast-moving traffic. Beyond that was the Fôret de Citeaux. To his left, on the side where he was sitting, lay the long line of hills which made up the Côte d'Or. The slopes were covered with vines as far as the eye could see. All those grapes! All that wine! It seemed strange to be taking leave of it already; so much had happened in such a short space of time. The town of Nuits St George flashed past, then Clos de Vougeot. Gevrey-Chambertin would be next. Any moment now and he would be able to see Clos Ambert-Celeste.

As it came and went Monsieur Pamplemousse wondered what, if anything, was happening there. It depended on whether or not the police took the shooting seriously. Ironically, they must have their hands full chasing the mythical rapist. The media would be baying for blood. The man's capture would have top priority.

There would be an inquiry about the shooting, of course, but such accidents happened all the time. As Boniface had rightly said, things would be far worse in the hunting season. What was the number of hunting deaths he had last seen for France as a whole? Some incredible statistic; the sort that made people shudder when they read it and then quickly forget.

Of the party of five who went out yesterday morning, only four returned, and they denied knowledge of exactly what had happened. A startled rabbit jumping out from under their very feet . . . all four had fired simultaneously. Dominique, Madame Ambert's brother – even more taken by surprise than the rest of them – had stumbled and one of the others . . . in the excitement it was impossible to say which one . . . must have hit him point blank.

It was plausible, possible even; these things happen. As plausible and as possible as the story of the tax inspector. If he'd been heading an inquiry Monsieur Pamplemousse knew the first question he would have asked.

At Dijon he joined the crowd heading for the subway and followed the signs indicating the locker area. Electronics took over again; rather more successfully this time. The machine dispensed a ticket with a computerised five figure number for the retrieval of his luggage. It even had the number of the locker printed on it. Monsieur Pamplemousse *conservé*d the ticket as instructed, putting it inside his wallet for safe keeping. To have his belongings incarcerated and miss the Paris train would be the last straw. He was suddenly anxious to get back home.

Twentieth-century technology struck another blow as he approached the great Burgundian Gothic cathedral of St Bénigne. Waterless restoration of the stonework was in progress; centuries of dirt vanishing in the ray from a tiny laser beam. The masons who had built it would have gazed in wonder and awe at the sight.

Signalling Pommes Frites to wait in the porch, Monsieur Pamplemousse entered the cathedral by the west door. Temporary rooms for the confessional boxes had been erected just inside. Both were locked. A notice listed when confessions were heard: between 16.30 and 18.30 on Thursday evenings, 16.30 and 19.00 on Fridays. Perhaps there was more to confess by the end of the week.

Following a line of arrows, he made his way down the right hand aisle until he found himself in a long passage leading to the sacristy. Paying his four francs entrance fee to an old woman in black seated behind a display of multilingual leaflets, he descended a circular flight of stone steps leading to the vaults.

He could have been stepping into Dante's Inferno. There were flash-guns going off in all directions; tourists everywhere – German, Japanese, Dutch, English. If whoever had written him the note had pictured their having a quiet *tête-à-tête,* he or she was in for a rude awakening.

Squeezing his way into the dimly lit nave,

past a group of Scandinavians peering down at what remained of St Bénigne's tomb, Monsieur Pamplemousse found himself inside a maze of columns, the centre area of which formed the base of the original Romanesque rotunda.

He stood where he was for a while, allowing the crowds to wash around him, hoping someone might make their presence known, but he waited in vain. Five minutes went by, then ten. He gave it another five, then made his way slowly back up the stairs. Perhaps whoever sent the message had been having second thoughts.

As he emerged from the crypt the woman behind the table glanced up from her cash register and beckoned to him.

'Monsieur Pamplemousse?'

'*Oui.*'

She handed him a note.

'*Merci, Madame.*' Ten francs disappeared miraculously.

The meeting place had been changed to one of the old confessionals; the first on the left after entering the cathedral through the main door.

As he approached it, Monsieur Pamplemousse felt as though he were committing a crime; a crime or a mortal sin. Was he expected to play the role of priest or confessor? Presumably the former. What if a genuine believer missed the notice about the temporary arrangements and sought absolution?

The answer to that was pinned on the board outside. Thursdays and Fridays only. Today was Monday. He could send them on their way with a clear conscience.

Choosing a moment when no one was looking, he pushed open a little half door and entered the double-sided box, pulling a red curtain across after him.

Inside it smelt of age. It was like being in a tiny wardrobe. He sat down facing outwards, wondering which side the voice would come from. Wondering, too, how many other secrets had been whispered over the years. What a strange vocation it must be, listening to others unfold their tales of weaknesses and woe.

A shadow darkened the screen on his right as someone entered the outer compartment. Monsieur Pamplemousse reached out and closed the shutter to his right.

The words when they came were hard to make out at first; muffled rather than husky. He guessed the speaker must be using a handkerchief.

'It goes back a long way.'

'Please begin at the beginning.'

'You were around in 1942?'

'I was around,' said Monsieur Pamplemousse. 'I was still at school, but I was around.'

'In that case you know the things that went on. Particularly in some of the *Lycées*.'

'The young are often rebellious, even if they are

not always sure what they are rebelling against. It is in their nature.'

'You know what happened here in Dijon?'

'At the school? Madame Ambert told me. There were live students arrested and only one was ever seen again.'

'Did she tell you my older brother, André, was among the ones who did not return?'

'No.'

'I worshipped him. He was all I ever wanted to be. Dominique Armand was the Judas . . . the one who talked. The others died because he wanted to save his own skin. When he came back after the war it was a while before the truth came out and when it did there was talk of revenge. He fled to America.'

'Why do you think he returned after all this time?' asked Monsieur Pamplemousse.

'Who knows? Greed? The thought of all that money which by rights he ought to be sharing. Things hadn't been going all that well. He'd got himself mixed up in one or two shady enterprises. Maybe he also had a yearning to be part of it all again. Some people feel a need to go back to their roots as old age sets in. Fifty years is a long time. He probably thought it had all been forgotten.'

'Revenge is sweet . . .'

'It is also a dish best eaten cold.' The speaker had dropped all pretence at disguising his voice now.

'Why are you telling me all this?'

'I want someone to know in case anything happens. If ever the truth comes out and I am not around for one reason or another I would like Madame Ambert to hear it from someone else's lips. Someone she can trust. She knows my brother was one of those who did not return, but she does not know the reason. I would like her to understand why I did what I did.'

Monsieur Pamplemousse thought back over the conversation he had had with her over lunch.

'She is no fool. I think perhaps she knows more than you think she does.'

'There is something else I must tell you. Something important you should know in case it ever comes out. It is to do with the shooting accident. Only one gun was loaded with live ammunition. The other three had blanks.'

'You mean...' Monsieur Pamplemousse considered the reply for a moment. Outside the confessional he could hear voices as a group went past. A flash went off. He waited until it was quiet.

'You mean it was a kind of Russian roulette; four guns and only one live round. No one would know who fired the fatal shot?'

'That was the intention.'

Something in the way it was said triggered off a thought in Monsieur Pamplemousse's mind. 'Who provided the ammunition?'

'I did.'

'And you made sure you got the round?'

'It was the loader's privilege.'

This time the silence said more than words.

'What will you do?' The question came at long last.

'I will light a candle for you.'

'*Merci*. You will tell no one?'

'I am not a priest,' said Monsieur Pamplemousse. 'I am bound by no vow of silence. However, nor am I any longer a member of the *Sûreté*. Your secret is safe with me. What happens after we say goodbye is between you and your conscience.' He hesitated. 'There is one question I must ask . . . Others may ask it too.'

'*Qu'est-ce que c'est?*'

'What happened to the rabbit?'

The box went quiet.

'An accident I can believe . . . a gun going off prematurely. But four experienced hunters all missing a rabbit right at their feet, that I would find hard to accept . . .'

There was another moment of silence, longer this time.

'*Merci*. There is someone coming. I must go.'

Monsieur Pamplemousse felt the light on his face as the shadow moved swiftly away. Footsteps came and stopped for a moment outside the box. He held his breath, then relaxed as they went on their way again.

He waited for a while before making a move.

Pommes Frites was restive again, pacing up and

down the pavement as though he had something on his mind. He looked relieved to see his master.

Monsieur Pamplemousse set off towards the Place Darcy, where he had seen a *Pavillon du Tourisme* on the way in. As it happened he found himself walking along the rue Docteur-Chassier. A little way along he stopped outside no. 9 *bis*. The gates were closed. Madame Ambert was right. There was no longer a plaque marking where the Gestapo headquarters had been during the Occupation. The building now seemed to be favoured by the medical profession. Perhaps it was just as well. Why commemorate so many unhappy memories?

He paused for a moment, gazing up at the windows with their net curtains. Fear of the unknown was perhaps the worst fear of all. Some people could manage that kind of thing, others couldn't. It was hard to picture how Dominique must have felt as he was marched inside, or to say what was right and what was wrong, or how one might have behaved in similar circumstances.

At the *Pavillon du Tourisme* he acquired a map of Dijon. The girl behind the counter was young, too young to know, or perhaps even care what had gone on. She conferred with a friend and together they directed him to where he wished to go.

As he approached the entrance to a small terraced park on the southern tip of the square, he came across a stone let into the wall commemorating the liberation of Dijon by Général de Lattre de Tassigny on the eleventh of September 1944.

Inside the park all was peace. Presided over by an unlikely-looking statue of a polar bear, the benches were mostly occupied by old men drinking in the sun as they listened to the fountains play or sat watching swans gliding gracefully to and fro in a small lake. Others had been commandeered by ladies taking a rest from their shopping, passing the time until their *autobus* was due. Here and there, young men and girls perched precariously on the back rails, gazing into each other's eyes for minutes, perhaps even hours on end. Obviously it was the current 'in' thing to do. Such behaviour goes in cycles.

Following the directions he had been given, Monsieur Pamplemousse found what he was looking for at last. Inside a building behind some iron railings he could see students hard at work; a teacher writing on a blackboard.

On a wall near the main entrance there was a plaque: 'On this spot in May 1942 five students were arrested by the Gestapo and subsequently deported to Germany. Only one returned.'

Someone had placed a single red rose on the pavement below the plaque. It looked freshly cut. Monsieur Pamplemousse bent down to count the petals; there were thirty-five, dark red and velvety. The scent was unforgettably that of Papa Meilland.

The plaque listed five names in alphabetical

order. Ambert, Dominique, headed the list. Then came Delamain, André. The other three names meant nothing to him, although he could guess their identity.

He wandered away from the school, aimlessly at first, in and out of the maze of back streets in the old part of the city, lost in thought; a mixture of anger at all the suffering caused by man's inhumanity to man, of so many lives cut short, and of so much waste. Pommes Frites trotted alongside, stopping every now and then to leave his mark. He, too, seemed lost in his own thoughts, occasionally sniffing the air as though looking for someone.

Monsieur Pamplemousse's meanderings took them past the *Halles Centrales* food market. It was nearly lunch time and the neighbouring streets were jammed with vans and lorries. Most of the nearby bars were doing a roaring trade as the drivers waited impatiently for the stall owners to call it a day. He wondered if Fabrice had been shopping for a rabbit.

A little way beyond the market he came across the vast bulk of the church of Notre Dame, with its rows of gargoyles and its three-bay porch. A little way along a side street a girl was having her photograph taken stroking an owl carved on one of the buttresses. He remembered reading that it was supposed to bring wisdom and happiness. It also reminded him of a promise he had made and he left

Pommes Frites to wait while he went inside to light a candle.

When he returned after a minute or two, Pommes Frites seemed unusually glad to see him. It was he, rather than Monsieur Pamplemousse, who led the way across the street and into a narrow, pedestrianised precinct opposite the church.

Suddenly, as they neared a small *créperie,* he stopped dead in his tracks and uttered a low, warning growl.

Monsieur Pamplemousse looked round quickly.

'You!' He made his way towards two figures waiting in the doorway of a bar. 'What are you doing here? What do you want?'

'A little information, that's all. Care for a drink?' JayCee nodded towards an empty table on the pavement.

Aware of warning signals emanating from Pommes Frites, Monsieur Pamplemousse shook his head. *'Non, merci.'*

JayCee shrugged, withdrew a pigskin wallet from his hip pocket, and began sorting through a wad of visiting cards. The one he selected bore the name of a protection agency with an address in Los Angeles.

Monsieur Pamplemousse cast his eye over it. It could be legitimate: it might equally well have been printed on a do-it-yourself machine in a local supermarket.

'You have problems with your job description?'

'You name it. I got fingers. The world is full of pies.'

Monsieur Pamplemousse slipped the card into his top pocket, then turned to Abeille. 'You do not look like a protection agent.'

'Jesus! There you go again. What *do* I look like? First you tell me I don't look domesticated. Then I don't look like a wine writer. Now it's I don't look like I'm into protection.'

'Listen,' JayCee interrupted. 'You had a meeting lined up just now. I want to know who it was with.'

'I am afraid I cannot tell you.'

'For Christ's sake, why not?'

'You wouldn't expect me to betray a confession?'

'Don't give me that crap.'

'I repeat, it would be a betrayal. There has been enough of that already. I am not in the mood to argue.'

'You can bend the rules. Once a cop, always a cop, right?'

'Why do you wish to know?'

'Let's just say it's a matter of some unfinished business. I owe it to a client . . . correction, an ex-client. OK?'

'*Non*,' said Monsieur Pamplemousse. 'It is not OK.' Reaching for his own wallet, he removed the pellet he had been carrying around and held it up for the other to see.

'Hey! Give me that.'

'*Jamais!* Never!'

JayCee made a lunge, then jumped back as Pommes Frites beat him to it.

'Anyway, so what?' he blustered. 'You've got nothing to connect me with that.'

'No?' Monsieur Pamplemousse replaced the slug. He was about to mention the tape which was locked away with his luggage at the *gare* – he didn't doubt that in the hands of an expert it would reveal more than he had been able to see – but he caught Abeille's eye. Reading his thoughts, she shook her head slightly.

He decided to take a chance.

'How about the evidence of the man who drove you to Beaune and back on the night of the pageant?'

It was a bullseye in one.

JayCee stared long and hard at Monsieur Pamplemousse. 'I could make you change your mind.'

Monsieur Pamplemousse looked around. The shops on either side of the street were thronged with people. Already those sitting outside the *café* were casting curious glances in their direction. Further along, near the entrance to the market he could see two *gendarmes* talking to a lorry driver.

'Here? In the centre of Dijon? The police would have your guts for garters, and Pommes Frites would finish up what was left. It is a long time since breakfast.'

'So, what do you suggest?'

'That you return to California. There are things here which are best left as they are.'

They stood in silence for a second or two, then JayCee gave a shrug.

'I guess you win some, you lose some. You can't blame me for trying.' Giving Pommes Frites a wide berth, he pushed past. 'Come along, Hunn.'

Abeille made as if to follow him, then paused. Pressing herself briefly against Monsieur Pamplemousse she gave him a kiss on the forehead.

'Thanks. You know something? Meeting you was a very life-enhancing experience.'

'I am not sure Dominique Ambert would say the same.'

'Yeah. You're right. But that would have happened anyway.'

'Who knows?'

'Hunn!' An impatient voice came from somewhere behind him.

'What is it you French say? *À bientôt*. Until next time.'

'In this case,' said Monsieur Pamplemousse, 'I think the correct word is *adieu*. It means goodbye.'

'*Adieu!*' As she went past he felt a tingle running down his back.

He didn't look back.

After a suitable interval he turned and headed in the direction of the *gare*. A clock was striking the hour as they made their way down the rue de la Liberté.

Pommes Frites, who was visibly more relaxed, drew his master's attention to a large *brasserie* in a nearby side street.

It bore all the signs. Starched white table cloths. Waiters speeding to and fro carrying heavily laden trays high above their heads, missing each other by a hairsbreadth, skidding to a halt on the polished floor. Baskets of fresh, crisp-looking bread. Vast floral arrangements. And if the view through the window was anything to go by, it was full of contented regulars.

The high desk by the revolving entrance doors bore the unmistakable patina of age. In its heyday it would have housed a *madame* in black bombasine keeping a watchful eye on all that went on; now it served as a repository for an assortment of credit card machines.

Spotting one of the last remaining tables, Monsieur Pamplemousse seated himself on a *banquette* between a potted palm and a heavily laden coat stand. Gazing round with approval, he gave Pommes Frites a congratulatory pat.

A Kir appeared, large, and of the correct proportion; a small ripple on the surface of Boniface's lake. It would have been a severe disappointment had it been otherwise.

He ordered a ham and cheese omelette, a green salad, and a *pichet* of red Côte de Beaune.

Afterwards, he shared a steak with Pommes Frites.

Looking at his watch, he called for *l'addition*. No doubt Doucette would have something special waiting for him when he got back to Paris.

The cordless credit card machine arrived at his table. He tapped in his personal number, pressed the validation key, and seconds later it accepted his *carte bleu* without question.

Monsieur Pamplemousse breathed a sigh of relief. All was right with the world again.

Theytarrived at the *gare* just as a cavalcade of motorcycles roared into the forecourt, escorting a small convoy of black Citroëns. Making for the left luggage lockers he found his way barred by an armed *gendarme* who demanded his ticket.

'What is happening?'

'*Monsieur le Président*.'

'Curiously,' said Monsieur Pamplemousse, 'I was thinking of him only yesterday morning. Perhaps he is here to see the *escargots*?'

'*Monsieur le Président* is just passing through.'

'*Quel dommage!* A pity!' It would have been something to talk about at the annual staff party.

The *gendarme* took a firmer grasp of his carbine. '*Et vous, Monsieur?*'

'Just passing through,' said Monsieur Pamplemousse sadly, as he tapped in his number.

'I am sorry to have sent you off on a wild goose chase, Pamplemousse,' said the Director. 'I gather from

248

Chantal's aunt that the problem at the vineyard has sorted itself out. It seems a pity that you chose to cut the holiday short. How I envy you the experience; the peace and tranquillity of it all . . . the total rest . . . all that food and wine.'

Monsieur Pamplemousse found it hard to find the right words. Some people seemed to go through life completely oblivious to the problems of others.

'I think it is possible, *Monsieur*, that had I not been there things might have taken a different course.'

Is that so?' The Director rummaged among some papers on his desk. 'Véronique asked me to give you this fax. It arrived this morning.'

Monsieur Pamplemousse glanced at the form. It was in response to a request he had made for information about the existence of JayCee's protection agency in Los Angeles. It read as he had expected.

'THE ANSWER IS IN THE NEGATIVE.'

'I do hate that kind of jargon,' said the Director. 'Why can't people just say no.'

'Some people find saying "no" is the hardest thing in the world,' said Monsieur Pamplemousse.

The Director looked at him keenly.

'Madame Ambert mentioned to Chantal that there was a girl involved. Is that why you have returned early? Was she . . . nice?'

'The answer to the first question, *Monsieur,* is again in the negative.' Monsieur Pamplemousse derived a certain amount of pleasure as he saw a look of pain cross the Director's face. 'As for her being nice . . .' He considered the matter for a moment.

'In some respects she was like no other girl I have ever met. Unclassifiable.'

'That means she was exceptional?'

'No, *Monsieur,* simply unclassifiable.'

'Aaah.'

'She told me she wanted *un baiser* behind the boundary wall of Romanée-Conti.'

The Director went into a state of shock.

'In July? When the grapes are reaching a critical stage? It could have been a costly affair, Pamplemousse. Think how much each vine must be worth. I shudder to think of Madame Grante's reaction had we been involved in litigation. Our P39 expense sheets would have been consigned to the PENDING tray.'

'I managed to dissuade her, *Monsieur.*'

'I am pleased to hear it. Did you . . . did you get to know her later?'

'Neither biblically,' said Monsieur Pamplemousse, 'nor in any other way. Although it was certainly not for lack of opportunity.'

Briefly, Monsieur Pamplemousse gave the Director a run-down on much that had happened, omitting those elements that were not for publication, concentrating more on the basics.

'You are saying the American was some kind of

hit man called in by Dominique Ambert to do away with Fabrice Delamain?' broke in the Director at one point. 'What is the world coming to?'

'Dominique was already involved in that kind of world. Having become convinced that it was his life or Fabrice's, and having seen undreamt of possibilities within his grasp, he wasn't going to give up without a struggle.'

'Was the girl deeply involved?'

'In the beginning I think she had no idea what was happening. She had simply gone along for the ride. I doubt if she had any idea what was going on until she came across a book – whether she came across it by chance in the boat's library or JayCee had it with him, we shall never know. The unlikely truth is that she was as simple and as genuine as she looked. A little like the film star Marilyn Monroe in that respect, and blessed with a figure to match. A child of nature who was streetwise enough to know instinctively which side her bread was buttered on. Insecure, and desperately wanting to prove herself. When she was told to keep me occupied she did her level best in the only way she knew how and got herself into even deeper water.

'Dominique had organised the pageant and booked JayCee and his girlfriend onto the boat. Not realising the kind of fellow-passengers there would be, JayCee thought up the idea of having her give a talk on wine to keep her out of the way. When he discovered my connection with the law he quickly tried to kill two birds with one stone by persuading me to look after her on the first night, knowing it would keep us both occupied. He hadn't bargained on his girlfriend unsuspectingly videoing the pageant. He also hadn't reckoned on Pommes Frites' ability to smell a villain a kilometre away and latch on to his being the thirteenth nun.'

'And after all that,' said the Director, 'Dominique has to go and get killed in a shooting accident. Life is very strange.'

'It is indeed,' said Monsieur Pamplemousse gravely.

'Talking of which, Aristide, I'm afraid I have some bad news.'

'Not another family crisis, *Monsieur*?'

'Worse than that, I fear. I have had a change of heart about the logo. It was triggered off by the finding of the *escargots*. As I said on the telephone it seemed an omen and the more I thought about it the more I began to feel we should take heed of the fact.

'One of the great strengths of France is her ability to embrace progress whilst at the same time retaining those things that have made her what she is; the old values.

'To cut a long story short, while you were away I faxed a number of our most important clients and posed the simple question: "Should we or should we not make the change?" Their answers were fed into our computer and the overwhelming vote is to keep things as they are.'

Monsieur Pamplemousse looked down. 'That is bad news, *Monsieur*,' he said gravely. 'Especially after all Pommes Frites has been through on *Le Guide*'s behalf.'

'I have the print-out here, Aristide, if you care to see it.'

Monsieur Pamplemousse waved it aside. 'Will you tell him, *Monsieur*? Or shall I?'

'He is your dog, Pamplemousse.'

'It was your idea, *Monsieur*.'

The Director tapped his desk top nervously. 'I wouldn't know how to begin.'

'In the beginning was the word, *Monsieur*.'

'How will he take it, do you think?'

'In some respects,' said Monsieur Pamplemousse, 'Pommes Frites has much in common with Abeille, the girl I have just been talking about. He has a simple approach to life. I think in his case he takes the view that there are few problems on this earth which cannot be cured by a good bone.'

The Director reached for his phone. '*Jambon* or *boeuf*?'

Glancing round the room in search of inspiration, Monsieur Pamplemousse's gaze landed on the portrait of Le *Guide*'s founder, Monsieur Hippolyte Duval. Was his imagination working overtime, or did he detect the merest hint of a smile on his face? Once

253

again, it could have been a trick of the light, or maybe merely a reflection of the gleam of anticipation in Pommes Frites' eyes. No matter what, the message from the latter was loud and clear.

'Perhaps a little of each, *Monsieur*?'

Pommes Frites didn't go quite so far as to nod his approval, but from the way he was licking his lips Monsieur Pamplemousse could tell he had said the right thing.

'After all, one way and another he has lost a lot of weight. He definitely needs building up again.'

Read on for an extract from
Monsieur Pamplemousse and the Carbon Footprint,
the most recent book in Michael Bond's
Pamplemousse and Pommes Frites series . . .

Monsieur Pamplemousse and the Carbon Footprint

MICHAEL BOND

CHAPTER ONE

Véronique put a finger to her lips before gently opening the door. 'If I were you,' she whispered, 'I would keep it low key. We're a bit edgy today . . .'

Murmuring his thanks, Monsieur Pamplemousse signalled Pommes Frites to follow on behind as they tiptoed past the Director's secretary into the Holy of Holies.

Glancing quickly round the room, he seated himself in a chair standing ready and waiting opposite Monsieur Leclercq's vast desk. Pommes Frites, meanwhile, hastened to make himself comfortable on the deep pile carpet at his feet.

Clearly, Véronique had not been exaggerating. All the signs suggested that if anything she was understating the situation.

Normally a model of sartorial elegance, the Head

of France's premier gastronomic guide looked in a sorry state; his Marcel Lassance tie hung loose around his neck, the jacket of his André Bardot suit was draped higgledy-piggledy over the back of a chair, and although one sleeve of the Eglé bespoke shirt was neatly rolled back above his elbow, the other looked as though it might have been involved in a close encounter with a lawnmower . . . perhaps while adjusting the blades, although that was highly improbable.

Unlike the past President of France, Monsieur Jacques Chirac, who was credited with having once operated a forklift truck in an American brewery following a spell at Harvard University, Monsieur Pamplemousse doubted if the Director had ever got his hands dirty in the whole of his life. The generally accepted opinion was that he probably laid out the ground rules at an early age; demonstrating clearly to all and sundry that even such mundane tasks as changing a typewriter ribbon were beyond his powers, making sure that letters dictated during the course of the day arrived without fail on his desk ready for signing at the appointed time that same afternoon. The licking of envelopes would have been someone else's responsibility, thus allowing his taste buds to remain unsullied by close contact with gum mucilage.

Discretion being the better part of valour, it was probably far better to hold his fire until a suitable moment arose. After what seemed like an eternity, and aware of a certain restiveness at his feet, he could stand it no longer.

'You sent for us, *Monsieur*?' he ventured.

'Yes, yes, Pamplemousse,' said the Director distantly. 'But it was you I wished to have words with first of all.'

Pausing as he riffled through the pile of papers, he glanced pointedly at the figure on the floor.

'Would you prefer it if Pommes Frites waited outside?' asked Monsieur Pamplemousse.

'No, no,' said Monsieur Leclercq gruffly. 'It's just that . . . well, to put it bluntly, Aristide, you are rather earlier than I expected and I have important matters to discuss. My mind is in turmoil and it is hard to concentrate when your every move is subject to scrutiny by two pairs of eyes rather than one.'

Ever sensitive to the prevailing atmosphere, and sufficiently conversant with the use of certain key words, Pommes Frites settled down again and, with his tail at half-mast, pretended to busy himself with his ablutions, although clearly his heart wasn't in it.

'Your message sounded urgent,' said Monsieur Pamplemousse. 'That being the case, we came as quickly as we could. It just so happened the traffic lights were green all the way. Such a thing has never happened before.'

'Aaah!' His words fell on deaf ears as an exclamation from the Director indicated he had at long last found what he had been looking for.

3

He waved aloft a crumpled form between thumb and forefinger. 'As you will doubtless remember, Pamplemousse, I recently issued a questionnaire to all members of staff.

'I had in mind ascertaining their views on various matters of importance. It was all part of an exercise in reappraising our current position in this difficult world of ours. Running an operation the size of *Le Guide* is a costly exercise, and from time to time, in common with most large companies, we have to take stock of the most expensive item of all: namely, manpower. It was our accountants who first posed the question. Are we, they asked, always getting value for money from those who work in the field?'

Monsieur Pamplemousse essayed a non-committal response, wondering what could possibly be coming next and fearing the worst.

'Cast your mind back,' continued the Director, 'and you may also recall the very first question on the list.'

'As a member of France's premier food guide, what are the three things uppermost in your mind at all times?' said Monsieur Pamplemousse.

In spite of himself, the Director looked impressed. 'That is correct, Pamplemousse. Which makes your answer, "Sex, money, and still more sex," singularly disappointing, even by present day standards.'

Monsieur Pamplemousse gave a start. 'But . . .' half rising from his chair, he held out a free hand, 'may I see that form, *Monsieur*?'

4

The Director smoothed the piece of paper carefully on a blotting pad before handing it over. 'I must confess, I was so incensed by your answer I screwed it into a ball and threw it into the waste bin. Unfortunately, my hand was trembling so I missed the target and it landed in a vase of flowers. The cleaning lady retrieved it for me later that day and left it on my desk to dry.'

'Where would we be without the cleaning ladies of this world?' mused Monsieur Pamplemousse, sinking back into his chair. 'Hortense is a treasure and no mistake.'

'Is that her name?' said Monsieur Leclercq. 'I had no idea.'

'Speaking from experience,' continued Monsieur Pamplemousse, savouring a minor victory, 'I venture to suggest the answer which so upset you probably reflects the view of the vast majority of the French population, the younger ones in particular. It is a characteristic of our nation that its citizens take the business of living and all its many and varied ramifications seriously.'

Holding the paper up to the light, he studied it carefully. 'Having said that, I must inform *Monsieur* that this is not my handwriting . . .'

'Not your handwriting, Pamplemousse?' boomed the Director. 'If it is not your handwriting, then how did it come to grace a form which has your name at the top?'

'That,' said Monsieur Pamplemousse grimly, 'is a question I shall address as soon as possible.'

A joke was a joke, but there were limits. He strongly suspected Glandier. The schoolboy in him was never far away. Blessed with a distorted sense of humour, his colleague's prowess as a performer of conjuring tricks at staff parties all too often extended itself to other forms of trickery when he was at a loose end.

'I accept what you say, Aristide,' said Monsieur Leclercq, 'albeit with a certain amount of reluctance.'

'It is an area where there are those who say I am accident prone,' admitted Monsieur Pamplemousse.

'Prone you may be while it is happening, Pamplemousse,' said Monsieur Leclercq sternly, 'but more often than not I fear it is no accident.

'That is why I fell victim to a jest that was in very poor taste. I am relieved to hear my faith in you is not entirely misplaced. The correct answer, as I am sure you will agree, is first and foremost the well-being of *Le Guide*, closely followed by carbon footprints and global warming.'

Monsieur Pamplemousse remained silent. He wondered how many of his colleagues lived up to such high ideals. As ever, the Director was out of touch with reality. Speaking personally, pleased though he was to know Monsieur Leclercq's faith in him had been restored, he could barely lay claim to always observing the first item on the list, let alone the other two.

'The phrase "carbon footprint" does seem to be on everybody's lips these days,' he said, non-committally. 'Next year it will doubtless be something else. These things tend to have a limited shelf life. The journals seize on whatever is currently in vogue and work it to death.'

'All creatures, no matter what their size, leave a carbon footprint,' said Monsieur Leclercq reprovingly. 'Whether by accident or design, it is a God-given fact of life and it is something that will not change. One must never forget that, Aristide.

'Centipedes, ants, earwigs, even the humble *escargot* . . . they all have their place in the scheme of things. They arrive on this earth hard-wired from the word go.'

Picking up on the phrase 'hard-wired', Monsieur Pamplemousse's heart sank. The words had a definite transatlantic ring to them. It suggested Monsieur Leclercq had just returned from one of his periodic trips to the United States. They often boded ill.

'I grant you,' continued the Director, 'that given its overall dimensions in terms of height, length and width, an *escargot*'s carbon footprint alongside that of, say, an elephant, is hard to evaluate.'

Pausing to sweep the pile of papers to one side, he leant back in his chair.

'However, it brings me to another matter currently exercising my mind, and which happens to be one of the reasons why I summoned you here today.'

Monsieur Pamplemousse listened with only half an ear. *Le Guide*'s logo – two *escargots* rampant – was a constantly recurring concern of the Director and there was little more he could contribute to the subject. Leaving aside the use of the words 'hard-wired', the phrase '*one* of the reasons' was also unsettling. It sounded as though there might be a whole catalogue of them.

Monsieur Leclercq picked up a silver paperweight cast in the shape of the subject under discussion.

'Apart from the fact that, strictly speaking, our logo is no longer politically correct, in many respects it no longer reflects the kind of dynamic image we need to project in this day and age, when the emphasis everywhere is on speed. This is particularly true when it comes to our readers on the other side of the Atlantic Ocean. In my experience, they are mostly blind to the humble *helix pomotia*'s virtues as a delicacy. Following considerable research, I have yet to see *escargots* feature on any American menu.

'However, that is by the by. The inescapable truth is that sales of *Le Guide* in the United States of America have plummeted over the past year.'

To prove his point he held up a graph showing a long red line which not only dipped alarmingly as it neared the right-hand edge of the paper, but disappeared entirely before reaching it.

'We are not alone, of course. Michelin have had their problems too, although they are fighting back. As you know, their logo has recently been updated. Monsieur Bibendum has shed a roll of fat and is looking all the better for it. He is now a leaner, fitter image of his former roly-poly self; and in so doing he has become an example to us all.'

'That kind of thing can backfire,' said Monsieur Pamplemousse. 'My understanding is that many people in America set great store by rolls of fat. They call them "love handles".'

'Is that so, Pamplemousse?' said the Director distastefully. 'I am happy to take your word for it.

'Be that as it may, our chief rival in the United States is a publication called *Zagat*, a guide that relies for its information on reports sent in by readers, who offer up their experiences when dining out. Given that more often than not they dwell on the size and quantity of fried potatoes, it is little wonder many of them have a weight problem.'

Monsieur Pamplemousse felt his pulse begin to quicken. Could it be that the Director was dangling a promotional carrot before his eyes? Head of the long-mooted American office, perhaps?

There would be snags, of course, but it was an exciting prospect. Pommes Frites would probably need to have a chip listing all his relevant details implanted somewhere or other on his person before being allowed into the country . . . that could be why the Director was choosing his words with care. He would know, of course, that Monsieur Pamplemousse would never contemplate going to America without him. It must also be the reason why he had been invited along to the meeting.

That apart, he wasn't at all sure how his wife would take the news. Knowing Doucette, she would be worried about what to wear for a start.

He tried dipping his toes into the water. 'For some while now Pommes Frites and I have been metaphorically girding our respective loins ready for our next assignment . . .' he began, hastily cutting short what he had been about to say as he realised the Director was still dwelling on the subject of snails.

'I fear the worst, Aristide,' said Monsieur Leclercq. 'Storm clouds are already gathering on the horizon for the gastropods of this world.'

'They come ready equipped to withstand any amount of sudden downpours,' said Monsieur Pamplemousse.

'It is not that aspect of it which bothers me,' said the Director. 'It is our image.'

'In that case,' suggested Monsieur Pamplemousse, 'could we not generate a little more publicity? A spectacular win in the field of international sport, perhaps? In *Grande-Bretagne* they hold an annual World Championship Race for snails. Last year's winner completed the 33cm course in 2 minutes 49 seconds and won a tankard full of lettuce leaves.'

'Hardly headline news, Pamplemousse,' said Monsieur Leclercq dubiously. 'In the field of sport it hardly ranks alongside the furore that accompanied the first 4-minute mile.

'Besides, a lot can happen to an *escargot* even in

that short distance. A passing blackbird could swoop down and make off with it long before it crossed the finishing line, and then where would we be?

'All that apart, my understanding is that supplies are dwindling. Many now come from as far away as Bulgaria. The climate changes we have been experiencing of late do nothing to help matters. The winters last much longer and they are growing colder. *Escargots* take anything up to six hours to copulate and even then it is very much a hit and miss affair.'

'I suppose,' mused Monsieur Pamplemousse, 'for an *escargot*, life is a matter of swings and roundabouts. Could we not use science to help them along? A little Viagra sprinkled on their lettuce leaves, perhaps?'

'I think not.' The Director gave a shudder. 'Who knows what might be unleashed?'

'In that case, perhaps it is time we changed our logo?'

'Change our logo?' boomed the Director. 'That is out of the question. Our Founder set great store by it. He would turn in his grave.'

Monsieur Pamplemousse took the opportunity to glance at the portrait of *Le Guide*'s Founder on the wall above the drinks cupboard to his left. Depending on the light, Monsieur Hippolyte Duval had an uncanny way of reflecting the prevailing atmosphere, but for once it offered no clues. Bathed in sunshine streaming through the vast picture window behind the Director, he looked extremely non-committal, almost as though he had washed his hands of whatever it was that was exercising Monsieur Leclercq's mind.

A passing cloud momentarily threw a shadow across the Founder's face, causing Monsieur Pamplemousse to decide 'fed up to the back teeth' might be a better description. Or, could it be that he was issuing some kind of a warning? It was hard to say. All the same, he couldn't help but agree with the Director. They must tread carefully.

'At all costs we must avoid doing anything untoward,' he said out loud. 'It would be a breach of faith.'

'*Exactement*,' said the Director, completely oblivious to the other's thoughts. 'However, we do have a fundamental problem in that *escargots* are, by their very nature, slow-moving creatures. From birth they are hardly equipped to exceed the speed limit wherever they happen to be going. They lack the get up and go spirit one associates with our friends on the other side of the Atlantic. Overtaking another *escargot* is not something that would ever occur to them. Pile-ups would be rife.'

'Could you not add wheels to the ones on our logo?' said Monsieur Pamplemousse. 'Or perhaps even mount them on a motorised scooter? The suggestion of exhaust fumes and the wearing of goggles along with bending over the handlebars would create an illusion of speed. Either that, or you could have them make use of one of those exercise machines with an endless belt. I believe they are very popular in American homes, and such an image could help no end with their carbon footprints.'

'This is no joking matter, Pamplemousse,' said Monsieur Leclercq severely. 'However, I do congratulate you for putting your finger on exactly the right spot as always. Mention of exercise machines happens to be particularly apposite at this juncture. I have already been toying with the idea of converting the bar area in the canteen into a gymnasium.'

Monsieur Pamplemousse sank back in his chair. It was all much worse than he had pictured. Such an idea would go down like a lead balloon. Strike action would be the order of the day once word got around.

'As you are well aware, Pamplemousse,' continued the Director, 'this is not the first time I have had to draw your attention to the fact that your own carbon footprint leaves much to be desired. As for Pommes Frites . . . his paws appear to have reached danger level. I hate to think how many units of wine he consumes on his travels.'

Monsieur Pamplemousse stared at the Director. How could he?

'With respect, *Monsieur*,' he said, taking up the cudgels on behalf of his friend and mentor, and with dreams of a temporary posting to America fading fast, 'dogs do not recognise units. I doubt if Pommes

Frites knows the meaning of the word. As for the size of his paws; may I remind you that they are attached to his legs and he has four of those in all. That being so, and notwithstanding the size of the whole, I venture to suggest his carbon footprint must compare favourably with the average *escargot*. It is like the old Citroën Light Fifteen. That, too, had a wheel at each corner and was much prized by the Paris Police for its weight distribution—'

'Legs . . . paws . . .' broke in Monsieur Leclercq, 'they are both problem areas and neither of you are alone in that respect.

'It is another area that is of concern to the accountants. The group insurance rate for our inspectors is the highest for the whole organisation. Only the other day, Madame Grante reminded me of the fact that according to the Association of Insurance Actuaries, the life expectancy of an average food inspector is less than that of a garbage collector in Outer Mongolia . . . her memo made depressing reading.'

'Most of Madame Grante's memos make depressing reading,' said Monsieur Pamplemousse. 'Besides, it is all very well for her. She hardly eats more than a mouse on a diet; her own carbon footprint doesn't bear thinking about. It must be the size of a flea's.

'As for those of us out on the road, sampling dishes across the length and breadth of France, I grant you weight *is* an occupational hazard. Two meals a day, week in and week out, may sound like a dream occupation to most people, but it can be quite the reverse. I count myself fortunate in having Pommes Frites always at my side, in a state of constant readiness to help out when required.

'Furthermore, if I may say so, the Association of Insurance Actuaries fails to take account of the fact that the "Silent Forks" column of our staff magazine, commemorating those who have passed away, has, over the years, been entirely made up of staff who were desk-bound. Since I joined the company no inspector has yet shed his mortal coil during the course of duty.'

It was a long and spirited speech, and even Pommes Frites looked up admiringly at his master when he finally came to an end.

'*Yet* is the key word, Aristide,' said Monsieur Leclercq mildly.

'Perhaps,' said Monsieur Pamplemousse, 'in order to ensure I am not the first, I should, for the second time in my life, take early retirement.'

Clearly, he had struck a nerve. The Director went pale at the thought.

'You mustn't even consider it, Aristide,' he said. 'Certainly not at this present juncture. I would hate anything to happen to you, and I am only speaking for your own good. Which is why . . .' he began playing nervously with the logo, 'which is the main reason why I have called you in at this early hour.'

The fact that from time to time Monsieur Leclercq had been using his given name hadn't escaped Monsieur Pamplemousse's notice. It was an old ploy. Get rid of various irksome matters first, undermine the opposition's confidence with threats of possible reprisals over minor matters, leaving them wondering what would happen next. Then, and only then, soften your approach. The Director was a dab hand at it. Not for nothing was he a product of a French *grande école*.

If past form was anything to go by, the true reason for their being summoned was about to be revealed.

'What is the best thing that ever happened to you, Aristide?' asked Monsieur Leclercq, settling back in his chair once again.

Momentarily thrown, and sensing he might unwittingly be trapped into doing something he didn't want to do, Monsieur Pamplemousse gave careful consideration to his response.

'Leaving aside the obvious things, like meeting my dear wife, I would say the moment when I retired from the *Sûreté* and they gave me Pommes Frites as a leaving present.'

'And the worst?'

'The day in the South of France when he disappeared into the Nice sewerage system and I thought he was lost for ever. If you remember, *Monsieur*, Doucette and I were taking a holiday in Juan-les-Pins. We had been planning to spend it in Le Touquet, but you very kindly suggested the change in return for picking up a painting in Nice on behalf of Madame Leclercq.

'It got off to a bad start when we had to witness a performance of *West Side Story*, given by the mixed infants at a nearby Russian School. Then, you may recall, that very same night a dismembered body was washed up outside our hotel, and from then on it was downhill all the way.'

Monsieur Leclercq gave a shudder. 'Please don't remind me, Pamplemousse,' he said. 'There are some things I would much sooner forget.'

'When Pommes Frites finally emerged,' persisted Monsieur Pamplemousse, 'he wasn't exactly smelling of roses.'

'May I ask what is the second thing which springs to mind, Aristide?' asked Monsieur Leclercq casually.

Sensing the other's disappointment and putting two and two together, Monsieur Pamplemousse essayed a stab in the dark. 'Undoubtedly the day when, quite by chance, we bumped into each other in the street,' he said. 'That, too, came about through Pommes Frites. We were taking a walk together.'

Monsieur Leclercq looked relieved. 'I don't know what I would have done without you all these years, Aristide,' he said simply. 'It was a happy chance that led us to meet as we did.'

'One turns a corner,' said Monsieur Pamplemousse, 'and one's whole life changes. I certainly have no cause for regret.'

17

'I have a big favour to ask of you, Aristide.'

'*Monsieur* has only to ask,' said Monsieur Pamplemousse, privately wishing the Director would get on with whatever it was he had in mind.

'Glancing through your P27,' said Monsieur Leclercq, 'I see that, apart from the many accomplishments you list, particularly those acquired during your time in the police force, weapon training and so on, you are clearly not without literary aspirations.'

'A great deal of my time in the Paris *Sûreté* was spent writing reports,' said Monsieur Pamplemousse. 'In some respects it is a very bureaucratic organisation. One always endeavoured to make them as clear and succinct as possible; marshalling the facts to prove the point in such a way as to leave no room for doubt. Defending lawyers are past masters in the art of ferreting out any loophole in the law.'

'Have you ever thought of taking your writing more seriously?'

Monsieur Pamplemousse shook his head. 'Since joining *Le Guide* all I have done is contribute a few articles to *L'Escargot*.'

'The staff magazine would have been all the poorer without them,' said the Director. 'I particularly enjoyed your last piece, "Whither *le coq au vin*".'

Monsieur Pamplemousse was beginning to wonder where the conversation was leading. It felt as though they were getting nowhere very fast.

'Apart from one or two outlying districts in

18

Burgundy,' he said, 'the dish is becoming more and more of a rarity. Its preparation is time consuming and, as you wisely remarked earlier, the emphasis everywhere these days is on speed. As for my taking up writing, that also requires time. And thinking time is becoming a rare luxury these days.'

'That being the case, Aristide,' said Monsieur Leclercq, 'how would you feel if I were to grant you a few weeks unofficial leave? Over and above your normal quota, of course,' he added hastily. 'Both you and Pommes Frites have been very busy on extra curricular activities of late. You could do with some quality time at home.'

'I must admit,' said Monsieur Pamplemousse, 'that when I first joined *Le Guide* I pictured leading a more tranquil life. In many respects, as Doucette reminded me only the other day, it has been quite the reverse.

'There was that unfortunate affair involving your wife's Uncle Caputo. His connections with the Mafia must be a constant source of worry to you.

'Prior to that there was the case of the poisoned chocolates . . . If you remember, Pommes Frites accidentally overdosed on some aphrodisiac tablets and ran amok among the canine guests in the Pommes d'Or hotel. It's a wonder people still take their pets with them when they stay there.

'Then, more recently, there was your unfortunate encounter with the young lady who was masquerading as a nun on the flight back from America. The one

19

who invited you to join the Mile High Club . . .'

'Please, Pamplemousse, I do not wish to be reminded of these things.' Monsieur Leclercq held up his hand. 'You have yet to answer my question.'

Monsieur Pamplemousse chose his words with care. 'The suggestion is not without its attractions, *Monsieur*. On the other hand, I find it hard to picture being idle for that length of time . . .'

'Oh, you won't be idle, Aristide,' broke in the Director. 'Not at this particular juncture. You can rest assured on that score.'

There it was again! Monsieur Pamplemousse's eyes narrowed. 'When you use the word "juncture", *Monsieur*,' he said, 'what exactly do you mean?'

'Really, Aristide . . .' Monsieur Leclercq brushed aside the question impatiently, much as he might dispose of an errant fly about to make a forced landing in his glass of d'Yquem. 'The word "juncture" simply underlines the fact that at this point in time we have reached a *moment critique* in our fortunes. A window of opportunity has presented itself, which, if all goes well, will provide us with a golden opportunity to hit a home run.'

Monsieur Pamplemousse winced. Anyone less likely than the Director to hit a home run in the accepted sense of the word would be hard to image.

'Am I to take it, *Monsieur*, that you have a solution in mind, and that I can help in some way?'

'That,' said Monsieur Leclercq, 'sums the whole thing up in the proverbial nutshell.

'I am not normally superstitious, Aristide,' he continued, 'but when I woke this morning and found not one but *two* blackbirds perched on my bedroom window sill, I feared the worst. I mistrust one blackbird, but two . . .

'Then, when my wife explained to me that not only was it a good omen, but a singularly rare one at that, I felt a sudden surge of excitement. It was a case of cause and effect. Chantal's enthusiasm was contagious. On my way into the office this morning the way ahead and the solution to our problems in America became clear.'

Monsieur Pamplemousse exchanged glances with Pommes Frites as the Director crossed to the door, made sure it was properly shut, then returned to his desk and, having phoned Véronique to ensure they were not disturbed, sat back in his chair and beamed at them.

The preliminaries off his chest so to speak, he was starting to look positively rejuvenated, almost as though a great weight had been lifted from his mind.

'I knew I could rely on you, Aristide,' he said. 'In fact . . .' breaking off, he rose to his feet again and headed for the drinks cabinet.

'I think it calls for a celebration. Some of your favourite Gosset champagne, perhaps? Or shall I open a bottle of the Roullet *très hors age* cognac?' His hand hovered over the glasses. 'The choice is yours. Which is it to be?'

21

Monsieur Pamplemousse hesitated. He was unaware of having even remotely agreed to anything. 'I hope you won't think I am being difficult,' he said, 'but without knowing exactly what we are celebrating it is hard to reach a decision.'

He should have known better.

For a brief moment Monsieur Leclercq looked suitably chastened. 'You are absolutely right, Aristide,' he exclaimed. 'I am so excited by the turn of events I am getting ahead of myself.'

He struck one of his Napoleonic poses; a pose honed to perfection over the years by taking in the view from his window of the Emperor's last resting place beneath the golden dome of the nearby Hôtel des Invalides.

'Pamplemousse,' he said grandly, 'I have a plan of campaign! It is my wish to run it up the flagpole and see if, in your view, it flies.

'If your answer is in the affirmative, then it is really a question of pulling all the right levers, and for that we shall need what is known as a road map.'

Monsieur Pamplemousse gloomily opted for a glass of champagne. It was a good buck-you-up at any time of the day or night, and he suddenly felt in need of one.

'Monsieur Leclercq has a plan?' repeated Doucette over dinner. 'I don't like the sound of that.'

'It is what he calls a "road map", Couscous,' said

Monsieur Pamplemousse. 'I must say I was a bit sceptical myself at first.'

'How many weeks will it take you?'

'That all depends on how many dead ends I come across,' said Monsieur Pamplemousse vaguely. He toyed with the remains of his dessert. 'It needs to be in place before the start of the racing season in Deauville.'

'It would never do to miss that,' said Doucette dryly.

'It is all mixed up with the annual staff party at his summer residence,' said Monsieur Pamplemousse. 'As always, wives are invited too, only this year, if all goes well, there will be an extra guest; a very important one.'

'July? That's over two months away.'

'Just think,' said Monsieur Pamplemousse. 'All that time at home.' He spooned the remains of the dessert onto his plate. 'Once again, Couscous, tell me the recipe for this delicious concoction. What is it called? *Crème bachique*?'

'Bacchus Delight,' said Doucette, 'is a baked custard made with half a litre or so of Sauternes, six egg yolks, four ounces of sugar and a touch of cinnamon.'

'But made with love,' said Monsieur Pamplemousse. 'That is the most important ingredient, Couscous.'

He gave a sigh of satisfaction. 'It is good to be home. White asparagus from the Landes with sauce mousseline – one of my favourites; sole, pan-fried in butter, seasoned with parsley and lemon and served with tiny new potatoes; and now Bacchus Delight . . . what more could any man wish for? Simple dishes, all of them, but as I have so often said in the past, anyone can follow a recipe. It takes love and understanding to bring a meal to full fruition. It is what is known as "the passion".'

'If you and Pommes Frites are planning to be around for two whole months, don't expect to eat like this every day of the week,' said Doucette, as she bustled around clearing the table. 'Besides, there are all sorts of things that need attending to. The window boxes could do with a thorough going over for a start. I will make a list . . .'

'First things first,' said Monsieur Pamplemousse hurriedly. 'It is a matter of priorities.'

'In that case,' said Doucette, 'I suggest you start by telling me exactly what Monsieur Leclercq has in mind.'

'Ah!' Monsieur Pamplemousse looked at his watch. 'Now that, Couscous, is going to take time. Time, and a measure of understanding. Perhaps, as an aid to digesting it all, before I begin we should open another bottle of Meursault? It involves my writing a play.'

Pommes Frites looked from one to the other before settling down in a corner of the room. A good deal of the conversation that day had gone over his head, but he knew the signs. Weighing up the pros and cons and coming down heavily on the side of the cons, it seemed to him his master might well be in need of support before the night was out.

If you enjoyed *Monsieur Pamplemousse Afloat*,
read on to find out about other books
by Michael Bond . . .

∽

To discover more great fiction and to
place an order visit our website at
www.allisonandbusby.com
or call us on
020 7580 1080

MONSIEUR PAMPLEMOUSSE
ON VACATION

Monsieur Pamplemousse is looking forward to a well-earned break in the South of France courtesy of his employer – all he has to do is collect a piece of artwork for *Le Guide*'s Director. But when his contact fails to show and a dismembered body is washed up outside the hotel, the holiday mood evaporates.

As Pamplemousse struggles with the case (and with modern technology) his ever-faithful bloodhound Pommes Frites is on hand offering proof why, during his time with the Paris *Sûreté*, he was one of their top sniffer dogs.

MONSIEUR PAMPLEMOUSSE
AND THE MILITANT MIDWIVES

It isn't every day that a coffin explodes during a funeral ceremony. Barely escaping with his life, thanks to a warning howl from his faithful bloodhound Pommes Frites, Monsieur Pamplemousse can only wonder who was behind the explosion . . . and if they were also responsible for the demise of the coffin's inhabitant.

But then another urgent matter comes to his attention: a terrorist group is planning to poison the food chain. Monsieur Pamplemousse, together with Pommes Frites and a rather strange ally, must spearhead an elite group to stop the catastrophe . . .

MONSIEUR PAMPLEMOUSSE
AND THE FRENCH SOLUTION

When Monsieur Pamplemousse gets an urgent summons from the Director of *Le Guide*, he knows that there is trouble at the top.

But neither he nor his faithful sniffer dog, Pommes Frites, expects the trouble to involve a nun who is in the habit of joining the Mile High Club or a full-scale smear campaign targeting *Le Guide*'s credibility as France's premier restaurant and hotel guide. Someone has been spreading worrying rumours among the staff and infiltrating the company files – awarding hotel prizes for bedbugs and praising egg and chips signature dishes. Even Pommes Frites has become a victim of the assault. It could all spell the ruin for *Le Guide*, but Pamplemousse is on the case . . .

MONSIEUR PAMPLEMOUSSE
AND THE CARBON FOOTPRINT

In an attempt to improve the lacklustre reputation of France's most prestigious culinary guide in America, the Director of *Le Guide* persuades Monsieur Pamplemousse to write a play for the guide's benefit, complete with a walk-on part for faithful bloodhound Pommes Frites.

Emphasising the importance of a healthy lifestyle to decrease one's carbon footprint, Monsieur Pamplemousse tries to impress the well-renowned American food critic Jay Corby, but disaster strikes on opening night and Corby storms out in a rage. It's vital he is found before he ruins everything for *Le Guide*. Luckily, star sniffer dog Pommes Frites is hot on the trail of their only lead: a flimsy undergarment belonging to an exotic dancer they came across in a state of undress before the start of the show . . .